I0525404

Remember Me

Michelle N. Onuorah

Remember Me
Published by MNO Media, LLC
Printed in the U.S.A.

Printed Edition ISBN-13: 978-0615992334
Printed Edition ISBN-10: 0615992331

This is a work of fiction. The characters, incidents, and dialogues are products of the author's imagination and are not to be construed as real. Any resemblance to actual events or persons living or dead, is entirely coincidental. The news world referenced in the book is entirely fictitious and has nothing to do with the real workings of ABC World News.

No part of this book – whether in print or in digital form – may be used, reproduced, or distributed in any manner whatsoever without written permission except in the case of brief quotes embodied in critical articles and reviews.

Please note there is occasional cursing, mild violence, and various references to sexuality and spirituality within this work of fiction. Reader discretion is advised.

Copyright © 2014 Michelle N. Onuorah All rights reserved.
Cover art © by Stephanie Mooney. All rights reserved.
Formatting by Polgarus Studio.

Scripture is taken from THE HOLY BIBLE, NEW INTERNATIONAL VERSION®, NIV® Copyright © 1973, 1978, 1984, 2011 by Biblica, Inc.® Used by permission. All rights reserved worldwide.

Scripture quotations are taken from the Holman Christian Standard Bible® Copyright © 1999, 2000, 2002, 2003 by Holman Bible Publishers. Used by permission.

Scripture is also taken from the King James Version of the Bible. (Public Domain)

Other Titles by Michelle N. Onuorah

Jane
Double Identity
Wanna Be on Top?
Type N

Available online.

CHAPTER ONE
Prologue

January 1st

"Ahh - get it! Get it, Caleb!"

The little boy with butterscotch skin quickly shot his rifle at the Terminator advancing towards his mother's video game character. He smiled up at his mom and watched in awe as she shot several other terminators in quick succession, all with a look of sheer excitement on her face.

"Take that, you evil monster! Ooh, a grenade!" Kristen aimed her remote at the gaming weapon and loaded up for the journey ahead. As she and her son played the Terminator Salvation video game, everyone else at Chuck-E-Cheese disappeared to them. They had laser focus on the screen in front of them, not even realizing their game had attracted the attention of several kids as well as parents.

Mark smiled as Kristen shot exuberantly at the screen. His wife always did have a way of garnering attention - whether it was at Chuck-E-Cheese or the studio at ABC. His smile dimmed a bit. It was a bitter reminder of her upcoming trip, scheduled only two days after their son's birthday.

She'll be fine, he tried to tell himself. *She's traveled before for special reports. She'll be careful and will return to us in four days. She'll be fine... But did it have to be Afghanistan of all places? Lord, please keep her safe.*

So deep in his thoughts was he that he nearly jumped at the feel of her arms wrapping around his waist.

"You okay?" Kristen asked in concern. He looked down at her and smiled.

"Yeah, I'm fine."

Kristen knew he was lying. She could tell when he was worried even when he tried his best to hide it. And she knew it was because of her upcoming trip. There were numerous things she loved about her job as a reporter - traveling used to be one of them. Now, it was becoming a dreaded aspect of her popular news show. She had traveled to all of Western Europe, much of Eastern Europe, India, China, South America, several nations in Africa from her ancestors' Nigeria to Tanzania, and even North Korea. She knew it was a rare privilege to say she had visited most of the world; but as she got older and her family grew larger, she knew that it was taking a toll on them all, particularly her husband.

She looked up at him and openly admired his chiseled jaw. Mark was tall, lean, and strikingly attractive. At six feet, four inches, he had a body that could easily bulldoze over anything in its path but he was graceful in all of his movements. He had thick dark brown hair that matched his dark brown eyes and his face was arranged with such symmetry and precision that Kristen often thought *Lord, you did good.*

His brows were creased in a worried frown again.

"Honey-"

"Mom, can we go now?" an impatient teenage voice asked. At fifteen, Jasmine was horrified at the idea of spending part of her holiday at Chuck-E-Cheese. When they'd first adopted her at six-years-old, she couldn't get enough of the place; but she had long since outgrown the center and was beyond done with the screeching children running around in obnoxious circles. Mark and Kristen looked at their eldest and were surprised to see that she had already read through the second novel she brought to the party. It had been three hours since they first arrived and they too were ready to leave.

"It's up to your brother," Mark said. "It's his birthday party."

"He's ready to cash his tickets," Jasmine replied.

"And Kylie?"

"YEAH!!!!"

All three heads whipped over to Kylie's exuberant cry. Worried expressions quickly dissolved into shock as they watched their four-year-old daughter jump up and down in the pile of tickets that flowed freely from the "lottery" machine. Caleb rushed up to them.

"Kylie won! She won ten thousand tickets!"

Kristen surmised, "Yeah, I think she's ready to cash hers out too."

The ride home was a happy one. Mom, Dad, brother and sisters couldn't stop chattering about Kylie's good fortune. The little girl was still grinning from ear to ear as she held tightly to the new Barbie doll her tickets had afforded her. The Barbie house and car were sitting in the trunk. Caleb was admiring the G.I. Joe his sister had been kind enough to get for him. Jasmine was busily recalling the look of horror on the management's faces at the sight of all those tickets...and the merchandise they had had to cough up in return.

"Mom, do you have to go?" Caleb suddenly asked.

Kristen sighed. It was the elephant in the car, and the house, and the party that everyone had tried to ignore. It was getting bigger each day her date of departure drew closer. For some reason this particular location was causing triple the anxiety. She glanced at her husband's profile and saw a muscle tick in his jaw. He kept his eyes on the road. She looked back at her three "babies" scrunched together with saddened expressions.

"We've gone over this, you guys. I'll be back in less than a week."

"But why does it have to be Afghanistan?" Jasmine asked, echoing Mark's earlier thoughts.

"That's where the wa—" she caught herself at Caleb and Kylie's expressions, "—the story takes place. It makes no sense for me to go to a different location if the story isn't happening there."

"I thought the war was ending." Jasmine said, refusing to censor herself for her siblings. Her mother glared at her but answered nonetheless.

"It is - which is why we're going. To give updates on how that's moving along and how the troops that are still there are doing."

She could see the concern etched on every single face in the car.

Kylie's small voice piped up, "Can we pray about this?"

"Again?" Kristen asked.

"Why not?" Jasmine countered. "You can never pray too much."

Kristen caught Mark grinning out of the corner of her eye.

She shrugged. "Touché. All right, let's pray."

She reached out her hands and watched as the kids linked up and bowed their heads. Mark kept his eyes on the road but glanced back at the rear view mirror, listening closely to his wife's prayer. When she finished her thoughts, each child took their turn and asked the Lord to protect their mother. They finished with a resounding "Amen!" and Kristen turned back around in her seat.

"Mom?" Caleb asked softly. She turned to him again. "You promise you'll be back soon?"

She smiled and said, "I promise."

Mark drove with one hand on the wheel and reached over to his wife's lap. He gently squeezed her leg before finding her hand and holding it in his own. She smiled at him and met his eyes. Their children had no idea what had just passed between them but it was the agreement of two lovers who were eager for their kids to go to bed.

Thankfully, they didn't have to wait long. The adrenaline of the win began to wear off and the birthday boy, exhausted from running around Chuck-E-Cheese, was soon ready for bed. Kylie's eyes were already drooping and Jasmine had resolved to get her "beauty sleep."

The minute Kristen securely tucked in their youngest, Mark took hold of her waist and swooped her up in his arms like a hat box. Kristen laughed.

"Wow, someone is eager tonight."

"You have no idea."

Fully satiated, Mark rolled over onto his back and pulled Kristen into his side.

"How long are you going to be gone?" he complained. She chuckled and stroked his chest softly.

"It's only four days. I'll be back before you know it."

CHAPTER TWO
Loss

March 15th – Two Months Later

Somewhere in the land between consciousness and slumber, Mark smiled, eyes closed, as he reached out to her side. He turned over as if to capture her beneath his arm and then woke up with a start at the feel of empty sheets.

He was awake.

The smile disappeared as he opened his eyes to the confirmation of what was not there. On the nightstand next to his wife's side of the bed stood the lone photograph of her in her wedding dress, smiling into the camera with a look of sheer joy. He reached out and pulled the frame to him. He caressed the lines of her cheek, the curve of her eyebrows with the very tips of his large fingers. It had become a sort of ritual to him; a way to comfort himself every time he woke up to the reminder that she wasn't there.

He sat up in bed, his hands still clinging to the frame. He glanced at his own nightstand and grimaced. The cards were stacked neatly in the order received, all from family and friends. He had yet to open the cards from the President, other dignitaries, or any of her fans - most of those were held in storage, waiting for him to retrieve them when he was ready. He looked at her photo again and like clockwork, that horrible day came shooting at him all over again.

The kids were scrambling around the house like that of a crew on a ship. Mark, their captain, issued orders on what chores needed to be done and what chores they could check off as complete.

"Okay, the upstairs bathrooms are done, the living room looks clean, you guys already did your bedrooms, so now we have to tackle the kitchen."

Jasmine groaned. "Oh, that's going to be fun."

"You want it to look nice for Mom, don't you?" Caleb pointed out.

"Let's do it!" Kylie declared with a grin on her chubby cheeks. Mark smiled at his youngest and led the charge.

For the first hour, they ignored the phones. So wrapped up were they in getting the house ready, they completely zoned everything out. But as they stopped to take a break, Mark noticed that the ringing wouldn't stop. He looked at the caller ID as the last call dropped off and saw that the caller had rung three times in a row. He pulled up the log and frowned at several other numbers that had called in repeated succession. Even more disconcerting were the caller names: all of them were from family and friends on both sides; the most frequent call was from the ABC producer in charge of Kristen's reporting special: Lance Carson.

He dialed Lance's number, stepped out onto the deck and pulled the phone up to his ear. Lance answered after the first ring.

"Oh, thank God! Mark, is that you?" a panicked Lance exclaimed.

"Yes, it's me. Lance, are you okay?"

There was a moment of silence on the other end.

"Hello?" Mark repeated, "Lance, are you okay?"

"You haven't heard yet," Lance stated in an eerily quiet voice.

Mark's heart dropped. Kristen. He tried to stay calm and kept his voice level.

"Heard what?" he asked. "What happened?"

Suddenly, he heard a rapping on the deck door. He turned around to see his and Kristen's friends, Reed Smith and Dierdra Cole, standing just inside the deck. He frowned at them in confusion. Why were they there?

"Lance, hold on."

He quickly reached the door and pulled it open. Almost immediately, he felt Dierdra enclose him in her arms.

"You haven't told the kids yet. Are you okay?" she asked in near tears.

He looked down at her with a perplexed expression. He glanced at Reed and told them both:

"You guys are scaring me. What happened?"

Their mouths dropped at his question. Mark pulled the phone back to his ear.

"What happened, Lance? Just spit it out."

"It's Kristen," he said without preamble. Mark sat back down on the deck step. "There's been an accident with the crew. Some sort of explosion and we've lost contact with the entire team."

If it was possible to feel all the blood escape from one's heart, Mark felt this was the moment it was happening. He heard a slight ringing in his ears and his palms began to sweat. His breathing was uneven, shallow, and he had to close his eyes to regain any semblance of concentration.

Father, no. Please, no. Not Kristen...

"Mark...?" He lifted the phone back to his ear. "Mark, nothing has been confirmed yet. I just wanted to tell you. Please, keep calm. We're going to get to the bottom of this and find out what is going on. Keep the kids away from the TV."

Mark nodded, although he knew Lance couldn't see him.

"I'll be here," he replied quietly. Lance hung up.

He could feel the eyes of both friends on his back. He stood up on shaky legs and turned to face them. Dierdra's tears had long since fallen. Reed looked at his friend helplessly and said:

"The kids are in Jasmine's room. We got them all to watch a movie."

Mark nodded in appreciation and walked past them into the house again, as though in a trance. He went to the living room, pulled the remote and turned to CNN. In bold letters, the headline appeared:

"KRISTEN TYVERSON AND ABC NEWS CREW MISSING IN AFGHANISTAN EXPLOSION."

Kristen's picture along with various reels of her past reports played on the corner of the screen while in the center, above the headline, footage showed the wreckage of the explosion site. Remnants of a large tankard burned on the wide dirt road as several soldiers and civilians scrambled around it. The reporter reappeared on the screen.

"For those of you just joining us, it has been reported that the vehicle carrying ABC World News anchor, Kristen Tyverson, and the film crew along with her, has exploded. Tyverson and six members of ABC news team, escorted by two soldiers, were in the middle of surveying civilian sites. Authorities have not released word on the status of any survivors. Details are unclear as to whether all members of the team were in the vehicle. Authorities are still trying to tame the flames and explore the wreckage."

The ringing returned to Mark's ears as he sat on the coffee table Kristen had chosen for the living room. He was dimly aware of Reed turning off the TV. He barely felt his friend grasp his shoulder. He could barely make out the words in his friend's prayer.

The rest happened in a blur. The same day Kristen was supposed to return home, authorities spent it digging through the wreckage and confirming the deaths of all those aboard. They did not find her body amongst the remains but made an official announcement presuming the deaths of all those who were a part of the reporting team. Accompanied by Lance Carson, two men - one in a military uniform, the other, a police uniform - offered Mark their condolences and left him the last of her effects. Mark would never forget the looks on his children's faces as he told them the news. Each of them responded differently. Kylie wailed in anguish, her small face crumpled in defeat; Caleb ran to his room and refused to open his door for hours. Jasmine quietly cried her grief. With Reed and Dierdra's help, Mark managed to pull them together and comfort them. A week later, they held a private memorial and funeral for Kristen and watched as ABC organized a public, televised memorial.

Present

Mark shook his head and tried to get the images of that time to disappear. It had been more than two months since her passing and he felt the same way he had the minute he'd received Lance Carson's call. He looked down at her portrait. The thought of her body gone, nonexistent, so completely obliterated by a blast that he didn't even have remains with which to bury…

Just two months ago, he had held her in his arms and made love to her. Just five years ago, he had watched her give birth to their daughter. He sometimes wondered if the authorities had been too quick to presume her dead. When he'd first received the notice, he looked for every possible alternative to her being inside of that tankard, especially when they hadn't found her remains. But they had gently reasoned that an explosion like that could vaporize any individual and that some of the crew remains were as little as twenty percent. At her funeral, they arranged a small grave and buried some of her possessions from the trip.

He picked up a card and tore the envelope open. From a distant relative, it simply read Revelation 21:4.

"…and He shall wipe away every tear from their eyes; and there shall no longer be any death; there shall no longer be any mourning, or crying, or pain; the first things have passed away."

A tear slipped down his cheek. And then another. And another. Something rumbled out of his throat from deep within; a cry of loss, loneliness, and shock. He dropped the card and folded the frame to his chest.

Hunching over, he wept.

March 15th - Afghanistan

She woke up with a start. The nurse in attendance had rudely shoved her awake. As Kristen stared up at the Afghan woman ordering her about in her native tongue, Kristen could do nothing but look at her in bewilderment.

"I'm sorry but I don't understand you."

She knows I can't understand a word she's saying. Why does she insist on bothering me before the translator gets here?

To her relief, the young Arab woman in her twenties strode into the ward and spoke to the nurse in their native language. The nurse gave her instructions, glanced at Kristen in annoyance, and left the cot without hesitation.

"Sorry, I'm late," Alima whispered. "How are you feeling?"

"Sore," Kristen replied. "Stiff. Still a bit weak."

"Your muscles have atrophied. Not severely but enough for you to notice a difference."

"How long have I been out again?"

Alima looked at her chart. "You were brought in on the eighth of January. The man who brought you here said you'd been unconscious for a day. You were in a coma from January eighth until February twenty fifth. It's now the fifteenth of March so you've had about three weeks of consciousness."

Kristen remained silent. Alima watched her closely.

"You still can't remember?"

Kristen shook her head.

"Well, you know your name." Alima pointed out. "That's a start. You know where you're from-"

"I just don't know how I got *here*." Kristen interrupted, disturbed. "I've never been to Afghanistan. The only places I've ever been abroad have been in Western Europe. What was I doing here? Where is my family?"

What year is it? Kristen thought the question but was too afraid to ask. She could read the concern in Alima's eyes and knew her memory loss was no joke but she didn't want to know the full extent of it yet. The last thing she remembered was celebrating her job appointment with her mom. She could still remember the disorientation when she first woke up, surrounded by strange faces, all of Middle Eastern descent. The air around her was hot, an arid heat she had never known before; as if it were two seconds away from emitting flames out of thin air. Her muscles had felt weak, her jaw stiff. Even worse, she couldn't speak the language with which the uniformed doctors and nurses were trying to communicate. For the first two weeks, Kristen survived on gestures, paying close attention to the pantomime of her caretakers as they helped her rehabilitate her stiff, wasting muscles. Both sides had learned rudimentary phrases to make the adjustment slightly easier.

When Alima had finally arrived, Kristen had almost cried for joy. But in that time, her presence there had only deepened the mystery. With no identifying documents or personal effects, the local clinic had no idea what to do with Kristen, short of treating her. The mysterious man who brought her in while she was unconscious had disappeared, leaving no contact information behind and Kristen could remember no such man. Even as Alima worked to get her out of the country, a screening process had to be followed, which included confirming her identity and ensuring she was well enough to travel. Given her atrophy and the physical effects from her injuries, the clinic's main priority was to treat Kristen to the best of their ability. That in and of itself was difficult because the clinic had the setup of a 1940s war hospital, with cots lined up back-to-back and no privacy to be found.

Kristen thought of her mom. Alima had tried to contact her via the number Kristen provided but the line was disconnected, confusing Kristen even more.

I need to go home. She'll help me piece the puzzle together.

"I need to get out of here," Kristen said. Alima looked back down at her charts.

"Alima, I've been here for three weeks doing physical therapy. When can I go home?"

"That's the problem, Kristen. I believe that you are an American citizen. You have the accent and everything but we can't find your passport or any evidence that you belong abroad."

Even worse, they could not find records of a "Kristen Johnson" ever having entered the country.

"Then what is the procedure?" Kristen asked.

"There are several documents that need to be processed. It's easier if you have an organization to leave with...which is why I'm having you transferred."

"What?"

Alima smiled. "Surprise. I found a local Red Cross stationed four miles away. They've agreed to take you. You'll have better treatment and an easier time communicating. You won't have to rely on a translations intern to get by. You can also get the travel clearance you need if they approve you."

Kristen closed her eyes in gratitude. She felt weak and drained and she had only woken up a few minutes ago but she was grateful. Grateful that she could soon get out of there and get to the bottom of everything that had happened.

It felt like months to her but five days later, Kristen found herself entering a new medical ward. This one was much cleaner with more space and advanced equipment. There were a variety of patients, mostly local civilians, who were receiving treatment. For once in over three weeks, Kristen was able to communicate seamlessly with several staff members, all of whom spoke English. She noticed that a couple of them took second glances at her and one even froze in astonishment but quickly recovered their expressions. She shrugged off the reactions as simple placement issues. How often do you see an African American woman walking around in Afghanistan in casual clothing? She knew she stood out.

She waited in a makeshift room drawn of nothing but standing curtains. After nearly an hour had passed, the curtain drew back and in walked a tall man with light brown hair and friendly blue eyes; those eyes became saucers the minute he saw her. His eyes swept over her in shock.

"I can't believe it," he whispered. "You survived. You actually survived."

She frowned at his familiar tone. "You know me?"

He nodded and said with a slight frown, "Reed Smith. Friend of the family."

She frowned at this but didn't argue. She had never met him before but she knew her mom had several friends she hadn't been introduced to yet.

"I'm a Red Cross medic out here for a mission. I honestly didn't believe them when they said you were here. Kristen, everyone had presumed you dead."

"My family thinks I'm dead?" Kristen asked.

"There was a funeral service and everything. How did you survive it?"

"Survive what?"

"The bomb. I'm assuming you were near it when it went off."

"That would explain the coma."

He looked down at her chart and nodded, finally understanding.

"I see you have some memory issues."

She nodded. "I know who I am and where I'm from. I just don't remember how I got here."

Reed nodded. "With an explosion at that close range, it's a miracle you're alive, much less with most of your memory intact. It's normal not to remember the moments leading up to your accident."

His mouth was poised to ask another question when the curtain ripped open and a young medic appeared.

"Excuse me," he told Kristen. He turned to Reed. "You're needed in ward four. Emergency amputation."

Reed immediately stood up. He promised Kristen he would return. Several hours elapsed before he did and by then, they only had time for a brief conversation. He initially wanted to contact her family and alert them of her safety but Kristen, in a burst of spontaneity, begged him not to.

"Are you crazy?" he asked. "Kristen, your family has been mourning your death for months. Don't you want to put them out of their misery?"

Her family consisted of her mother and distant relatives she had only met once in a blue moon. *He must mean my mom and close friends,* she thought. Well, as far as she was concerned, her friends could wait. Her mom, she wanted to surprise. She could only imagine the look on her face when she realized her daughter was actually alive. So she insisted and eventually, Reed complied.

In five days' time, though they barely spoke to each other between his other responsibilities and her physical therapy, Reed managed to arrange for

Kristen's travel clearance. They left together in a Red Cross-appointed helicopter, returning to the States without any fanfare or struggle. When they arrived on U.S. soil, Kristen allowed Reed to do all of the paperwork and all of the talking. Landing on a private airfield helped the process immensely.

CHAPTER THREE
Reunited

*March 25*th

Kristen could hardly contain the excitement coursing through her body. After her ordeal, she was relieved to finally see the familiar surroundings of Atlanta, Georgia. As Reed drove past the city structures and into the suburban part of town, she began to imagine the expression on her mother's face when she realized that she was alive. Sure, she'd probably smack her once she learned of how long Kristen had kept it a surprise and she would probably call her daughter out for being so selfish but Kristen couldn't help but see for herself the shock and relief that would cross her mother's face.

Kristen thought it odd that they were driving into Buckhead – the most affluent part of town. Did he have to make a stop before taking her home? Reed entered a quiet subdivision that she didn't recognize but it wasn't until he pulled up to a large, brick-front house that Kristen voiced her confusion.

"Where are we?"

Reed looked at her, a slight look of confusion crinkling his eyes.

"Your home." Before she could respond, he slid out of the car and opened her door.

"Come on, let's see your family."

They made it half way across the lawn before the door burst open and a tiny, little biracial girl sprinted out of the house and into Reed's arms.

"Uncle Reed!"

"Kylie! How's my little munchkin?" But Kylie had stopped listening. She froze stock still in Reed's arms as she looked over his shoulder. An older biracial girl in her teens crossed the threshold, a look of irritation and worry mingled on her face.

"Kylie, how many times have I told you not to just burst out of the hou-"

She stopped mid-sentence, staring at Kristen, eyes wide. A shorter boy with cafe-au-lait skin appeared beside her.

"Mom?"

Kylie had recovered. She shoved herself out of Reed's arms, landed on her feet and sprinted over to Kristen.

"Mommy!"

The boy and teenage girl quickly followed. They embraced her as if she were life itself. Kristen stood still as the children invaded her space and grabbed at her waist.

Kristen frowned at Reed in confusion and Reed's smile slowly disappeared. Why was she reacting this way? He looked closer at her and the realization slowly started to take shape.

"What's going on out here?" a deep, baritone voice called out. The teen pulled back from Kristen a fraction of an inch and turned to the brown haired, brown-eyed man at the threshold.

"Dad, she's alive. She's alive!"

But he had already registered that. A look of complete astonishment was written on his handsome face as Mark crossed the lawn. He didn't know that his feet were running. He didn't know that Reed stood on the lawn. He could barely register the tears that blurred his vision and ran down his cheeks.

His children parted slightly from their mother's form as he reached her and drew her tightly into his arms - so tightly, she felt as though her ribs were about to break. His hands reached up to cup her face as he bent down and kissed her soundly on the lips. Only when she yanked back, eyes wide, did he and those around him snap out of it.

Kristen looked at the people in front of her in horror before turning her gaze to Reed's.

"Where is my family? *Who are these people?*"

Oh my God. Reed thought in horror. *She really doesn't remember them.*

He wanted to tell himself he was being ridiculous. That of course she remembered her own husband and children but as she looked around at all of them in horror and confusion, as though *they* had lost their minds, he knew she had no recollection of the people gathered around her. Again, she looked at Reed.

"Where is my mother?" she asked warily.

Their mouths dropped. The two older kids gave each other strange looks. Mark glanced at Reed in concern.

"Grandma?" Kylie asked in confusion. "Mommy, Grandma-"

Mark quickly cut her off with, "Jasmine, take your brother and sister inside."

The teen with massive tawny curls looked between her parents before escorting her siblings inside.

"I wanna stay with Mommy," Kylie whined, almost in panic. The boy had long since gone quiet, his smile replaced by a chilly veneer. He grabbed his little sister's hand and pulled her into the house behind his older sister without a backward glance.

Jasmine reassured her, "You'll see her again soon."

Kristen frowned. These people were under the impression that she belonged with them, that she was the wife and mother missing from the equation. This was a mistake. It had to be. She probably looked very similar to these kids' mom and they swarmed her because of it.

But what about the man?

Kristen pulled her gaze away from the house only to find him staring at her with a look of longing and absolute joy. He looked her up and down with eyes that missed nothing and his tears had long since fallen. He was handsome with thick cognac hair that matched his eyes. Muscular and toned, he was more than a head taller than her and she stood at five feet, ten inches. She guessed that he was probably around six four.

"What happened?" he asked Reed, but kept his gaze fixed on her.

"She was transferred to my ward two weeks after I had arrived. They said she'd been in a coma for over a month and was in the middle of physical therapy when the patient overflow and language barrier required a move."

Kristen shifted uncomfortably under the stranger's blatant assessment of her. He looked at her intimately as if he knew her body just as well as she did. She didn't know what was more disconcerting: this man's gaze or the fact that Reed was sharing her medical history with him.

"How was she injured?"

"A bomb," Kristen spoke up. "Reed said my team got caught in the crossfire but that doesn't make any sense."

She turned to Reed. "I've wanted to ask you: why would KJLH be in Afghanistan? We only cover local news."

"Kristen," the brown-haired man began quietly. "What year is it?"

She frowned at the question and looked between the two men. It was the same question she had avoided in Afghanistan and on the journey back home. It was the question she had wanted to ask her mother, who would explain everything if she was wrong. Reed was silent with an air of apprehension. Both men waited for her to answer.

"2003," she said forcefully, as though willing her assertive tone to make it correct.

The dark-haired man's face fell instantly. Reed looked crestfallen.

"Kristen?!" a loud voice called across the street. They all turned to see a plump redheaded woman stride across the street with the full intention of embracing the newly returned neighbor. Mark stepped in front of Kristen, shielding her.

"Hi, Janet. Listen, right now is not a good time." But the woman wasn't listening. She craned her neck to try and get a view of Kristen.

"That is her, right? What happened? I thought she was presumed dead? Oh, Mark, I'm so happy for you! Do the kids know?"

Kristen was about to have a meltdown. She felt as if she were in the twilight zone. As Mark responded to the neighbor, she hissed at Reed, "Get me out of here."

Reed looked at her and could see she was reaching her limit.

"I can't just take you-"

"Where is my mother?"

"I think we should-"

"Where is my mother?" she repeated more loudly.

"Oh my God, she really can't remember?" Janet voiced behind her. Kristen turned and surveyed the woman with kind eyes.

"Who are you? Do you know my mother? Thelma Johnson?"

Janet looked from Kristen to Mark and over to Reed.

"Why won't anyone tell me what's going on?!" Kristen exclaimed.

Janet and Reed looked flummoxed.

"Let's go inside," Mark said firmly. He turned to Kristen. "Don't worry, we're gonna take you to the living room and explain everything to you." He stepped up and cupped his hand around her elbow. He noticed that she stiffened at his touch but she didn't pull away.

They crossed the lawn and entered the massive, warmly decorated house. Kristen gasped instantly at the sight of a framed portrait fixed in the center of the hall. There she sat with the stranger and his children, surrounding her as she smiled warmly into the camera. Immediately to the left, stood a formal living room and, seeing her shocked expression, Mark gently ushered Kristen over to one of the plush sofas. He turned to Janet and asked:

"Would you mind keeping an ear out for the kids? I don't want them to come in just yet and I think they've had a bit of a shock."

Janet nodded and immediately left down the hallway, as though she knew the very layout of the house. The house that Kristen was supposed to know inside out if what these people said had any credence to it.

Mark and Reed sat opposite her and finally got to the point.

"Kristen," Reed began. "I don't know how to put this so I'll just say it straight. It appears that you have suffered from a severe case of amnesia."

She'd gathered as much.

"The year is not 2003," Reed continued. "It is 2014."

"What?" Kristen shot up indignantly but sat back down at their sober expressions.

"What?" she repeated quietly in horror. When she first saw their reaction to her calendar estimate, she knew she had stated the wrong year but she thought at worst maybe she was a couple years off. Not *eleven*. The room became a little less clear and her breathing a little more shallow. She looked down at her lap as she began to feel queasy and didn't know what to do.

"Breathe." She heard a warm whisper in her ear and a strong hand stroke her back.

It was him. The stranger who kissed her on the lawn. She followed his instruction and took a few deep breaths as the room began to still. He had a calming presence and it concerned her that he made her feel so at ease.

When she recovered she kept her gaze on her lap and asked quietly, "Who are you?"

Mark looked at Reed and he nodded his approval.

"My name is Mark Tyverson and I'm your husband - breathe...breathe."

The hand at her back gently pushed her forward so that she bent her head between her legs and breathed deeply yet again. Though she didn't want it to, it started to make sense. A Kristen Johnson hadn't entered Afghanistan because a Kristen *Tyverson* had.

Eleven, she thought. *Eleven years. How can I not remember eleven years?* She struggled in vain to mentally grasp at the missing memory, the same way a person would try to remember a passing thought. As if it could come that easily. No. The last thing she could remember prior to waking up in that hospital was celebrating her job appointment at KJLH with her mom over dinner.

"Mom," she said. Her head rose again. "Where is my mom?"

She'll explain everything to me. She'll help me catch up.

But as Kristen looked at the somber faces around her, she felt a sense of foreboding. Mark scooted closer to her and felt her stiffen again. It stung him but he ignored it, acknowledging that, to her, he was still a stranger. His hand still on her back, he grasped one of her hands with his free one and broke the news without preamble.

"Your mom passed away two years ago from ovarian cancer. I'm so sorry, Kristen."

Even though he had tried to brace himself for her response, nothing could have prepared Mark for Kristen's reaction. She leapt off the couch and away from him, as if he were acid. As if his very words had scalded her. She didn't say anything but shook her head vehemently as if she could shake that reality away, all the while her eyes welled with tears. Mark stood to slowly approach her but she immediately found her words.

"Stay away from me." she said suddenly, her hands braced in front of her.

"Kristen," Mark persevered. "I know this hur-"

"Stay away from me!" she screeched adamantly.

Reed stood up, "Mark, don't."

Mark turned to him and frowned. "She needs me."

"She doesn't know you." He tried to soften the blow with, "She's in too much shock to accept your comfort."

Reed turned to Kristen and slowly approached her, which she allowed. Mark tried to push back the feelings of jealousy…inadequacy…as he watched his wife grant another man permission to touch her. Reed gently grasped her elbow and led her back to the couch. He spoke in soothing tones and rubbed her back as she gave in to the grief that had enveloped her two years ago. Only this time, it was amplified by shock and loneliness.

Mark watched helplessly as Kristen sobbed into Reed's shoulder. He heard shuffling behind him and turned to see Jasmine looking on in despair. She made a move to approach her mother but stopped when Mark raised his hand and shook his head. She nodded and quietly left the room. When Kristen's sobs began to subside, Reed looked up at Mark and quietly asked:

"Does she have any other family of origin?"

Mark shook his head.

"Close friends? Anyone who knew her longer than eleven years - even before she met you?"

"Dierdra."

The name left his mouth almost immediately and Reed nodded.

"Of course," Reed replied. "How could I forget?"

Kristen's head snapped up. "Dede?" she gasped and met her husband's eyes for the first time in minutes. "You know Dede?"

"She's your best friend."

"Yes, I've known her since high school. Where is she?"

But Mark was already taking out his cell phone. "I'll call her right now."

"Oh my God, I can't believe this! Thank God you're alive!" Dierdra spoke into her ear as she squeezed Kristen close to her. Kristen squeezed just as hard. She was relieved to finally see a familiar face; and was eager to learn about everything she'd missed out on from a source she could trust.

They stood in the middle of the formal living room. Janet had long since taken the kids outside to play. There was no chance of eavesdropping. Mark and Reed stood to the side as the two friends embraced. When they separated, Dierdra brought Kristen back over to the love seat and sat beside her. She glanced at Mark, nodded, and turned to Kristen.

"So your hubby tells me you don't remember much."

"So he *is* my husband?" Dierdra's eyebrows shot up in surprise. Reed glanced over at Mark only to find him grinning slightly. This was just like her. To question everything until she felt it was coming from a credible source.

"Yeah, boo! You two have been married for over ten years. I was the maid-of-honor, of course."

Kristen glanced at Mark surreptitiously but couldn't hold his gaze. He was watching her with an intense look that she had no idea what to do with. She looked into her best friend's eyes.

"You like him?"

Dierdra nodded.

"Mom likes...*liked* him?"

She could feel tears welling in her eyes as her friend squeezed her hands and said softly:

"She called him her son."

At this, Kristen glanced at him. Mark looked down at his shoes at the mention of his late mother-in-law. He missed her too.

Dierdra grabbed her attention again.

"Honey, I don't know all the details Mark and Reed gave you but whatever they told you, I assure you it's true. You've been married to Mark for ten years. One year into your marriage, you adopted Jasmine who was six at the time. She's now fifteen. Caleb is nine and Kylie is five. You gave birth to both of them."

Kristen laughed incredulously. "I gave birth?"

She placed a hand on her womb as though she couldn't believe two humans had come from there without her recollection. She dipped her head back into her hands. She was overwhelmed again.

Dierdra looked at the two men standing before them.

"Can you guys give us a moment alone?"

Mark looked reluctant to leave but Reed placed a hand on his shoulder and guided him out. Mark kept his gaze fixed on Kristen as Dierdra assured him, "I'll only be a second. Don't worry."

Dierdra turned back to Kristen and saw her shoulders shake softly. She was crying. She pulled her into her arms.

"Krissy, it's okay," she said softly.

"No, it's not. Why? Why is this happening, Dee? The last thing I remember is having dinner with Mom after I got my KJLH gig. How in the hell could I forget *eleven years* of my life?"

"That must have been some serious bomb."

Kristen raised her head and looked at Dierdra's deadpan expression. She didn't know whether to slap her or laugh. She chose the latter and Dierdra joined in.

"You're such an asshole sometimes."

"I know, I'm sorry. I just wanted to see you laugh. Krissy, I know this is hard. Harder than anything I can imagine but look at the bright side. You have a wonderful life. You have a husband who adores you, three beautiful children, and an amazing career."

"I'm a local anchor. How is that an amazing career?"

"They didn't tell you?"

Kristen frowned. "Tell me what?"

"Kristen, you haven't been a local anchor since 2005. You are the first and only black woman to anchor *World News*."

"What?!" Kristen shouted. "*World News*? *ABC World News*? The globally televised *World News*?"

Dierdra grinned and nodded, pride stamped all over her face.

"You did it, girl. You made your way into the upper echelon of journalism. You are the recipient of *four* NAACP Awards for Outstanding News, two Emmys, and a Pulitzer Prize nominee."

"Entrant," Kristen corrected.

"Nominee," Mark answered. He and Reed had returned after hearing her outburst. "You are the most popular journalist since Katie Couric stepped down from reporting."

"Whoa, whoa, whoa. Couric is no longer reporting?"

"She has her own talk show now," Reed answered.

"Which just got cancelled," Dierdra added.

Floored. She was floored. Kristen sat back down and took deep breaths again. Mark watched her closely and finally said, "Can you both give Kristen and me a moment alone, please?"

Kristen looked up in confusion, almost panic, and it hurt him to see that expression at his mere request to be alone with her. But he refused to back down. His expression uncompromising, Reed and Dierdra left the room as Reed began to tell Dierdra more details about the accident.

Kristen didn't know what to do.

She looked at her hands, then the floor, then the furniture around her. When she finally looked back at him, she found him staring at her as though he had been waiting for her to finally meet his eyes. A tender expression filled them and she knew this man loved her…whoever he knew her to be. He slowly walked over to her and took Dierdra's place on the love seat.

"How are you?" he asked gently.

He was the first person to ask her that since she found out. And she knew he wanted a straight answer.

"Not so good," she admitted. He nodded in understanding.

"Tell me what's going through your mind."

She shrugged. "Where do I start? I wake up thinking I'm a twenty-six-year-old virgin who is just starting out her career and now I find out I'm…what, thirty-seven?"

He nodded. She blew out some air as the shock sunk in.

"I'm thirty-seven, have three children, am married to someone I don't remember ever seeing in my life - no offense."

"None taken." He smiled.

"On one hand, I should be grateful that my life has turned out relatively well. On the other hand, I'm pissed because I missed it all. And my - my mom…" she started choking up.

Mark gently pulled her into his side, once again rubbing circles on her back. It was really soothing and even though she didn't know this man, his presence calmed her down when she wasn't thinking about the fact that she didn't know him. She felt more than heard the rumble in his deep voice as he gently spoke against her hair.

"'The Lord is my shepherd. I shall not want. He maketh me to lie down in green pastures. He leadeth me beside the still waters. He restoreth my soul. He leadeth me in the paths of righteousness for His name's sake. Yea, though I walk through the valley of the shadow of death, I will fear no evil for thou art with me. Thy rod and thy staff, they comfort me…'"

He recited the entire psalm from memory in the deep, comforting tone that eased her soul. He was a Christian. Thank God for small favors. They sat in the still room and let the comfort of the psalm sink into both of their spirits. After a while, Kristen pulled back.

"What now?" she asked him and he was ready.

"You're staying here with us. I already called a specialist and we'll see him tomorrow to find out more about your memory loss. I also called our therapist."

She frowned. "A therapist? We have a therapist?"

He nodded, wary. "We've been seeing her for three years now."

"Why? What's wrong with our marriage? Were we about to divorce?" She pulled back from him in suspicion.

He shook his head in surprise. "What? No. No, our marriage is fine. It just helped us to communicate better."

Kristen shook her head. "I'll see the specialist but I'm not interested in a shrink."

He was frustrated but not surprised. "You resisted seeing her for over a year before you decided to go with me. She really helped us a lot."

"Yeah, and now it's all for nothing because I can't remember any of it."

"She can help us again."

"I said no. I don't like shrinks."

He knew that. And he knew why. But he thought better than to push it at that very moment.

He nodded. "Okay, let's just get you settled for tonight and take things one step at a time. I think that'll be less overwhelming for you."

She nodded.

"If you're up to it, I can give you a quick tour of the house and you can decide where you want to sleep."

She nodded but avoided his eyes. She was still nervous around him. Mark told Reed and Dierdra of the game plan and thanked them for their help. Janet had left shortly before Reed and Dierdra did. Dierdra hugged Kristen goodnight and promised to check on her the next day. Reed did the same for Mark. As they headed out to their cars, Kristen couldn't help but feel a sense of apprehension as the two people she knew left her with a person she felt completely foreign around. If Mark thought she was quiet before, she was downright mute when their friends left.

Asking Jasmine to watch the kids again, he made the tour as quick as possible. He could tell she was drained, still overwhelmed, and in the middle of grieving her mom. He explained the layout of the five bedroom home. All the rooms were upstairs, there was a basement and an attic and a deck with an expansive yard beyond it. The kitchen was state of the art, with all modern appliances and finishes. The home was built according to their specifications six years ago, when they were expecting Kylie. Kristen couldn't believe she owned such a large estate. It was a mansion compared to the tiny one bedroom apartment she leased 11 years ago. Of course, to her, it felt like just yesterday she was bumping her way through the cramped space.

He ended the tour at their master suite.

"This is our room," he said as he pushed the double doors open. The suite was the creme-de-la-creme of the house. Spacious with a walk-in closet so large, it could double as an additional bedroom, the four post king-sized bed took center stage. It had already occurred to Kristen on more than one occasion that she and this man had shared that bed, had been intimate on that bed. She could only imagine the things they'd done with and to each other on that bed that she had no recollection of but he knew completely. As she stood and looked at it, she couldn't bring herself to meet his eyes, lest he guess what she was thinking.

He already knew. He took one look at her face eying the bed and had to restrain his own longing in response.

He gently said, "I want you to feel comfortable. You can sleep in this room or in the guest room. I'll make myself scarce either way. All of your belongings are still here, just as you left them."

She appreciated his consideration. Not that she was expecting him to force himself on her but the fact that he unquestioningly gave her space meant a lot to Kristen.

She kept her gaze fixed on the bed and answered, "I'll stay in the guest suite. Thank you, though."

He nodded understandingly and walked to their massive closet. He picked out several garments, intimate wear, towels, and toiletries and strode to the guest bedroom. She entered the room as he placed them on her bed.

"These should make you more comfortable. They're your favorites. There's an adjoining bathroom here so you'll have complete privacy." He held the back of his neck in thought and finally met her eyes. "Just let me know if you need anything else. I'll be right down the hall."

She nodded.

His eyes turned tender and, deeply affected, he whispered, "I'm so grateful you're back."

He looked down as tears began to well. Kristen didn't know what to say. She didn't want to embarrass him and she didn't know how to respond to his feelings. He spared her the predicament, though, by quickly kissing her forehead and making his exit.

As soon as he left and closed the door behind him, the pitter-patter of little feet ran up the stairs and over to the outside of her door.

"Where's Mommy?" Kylie demanded.

She heard Mark speak softly through the door. "Mommy's really tired. She needs to sleep. You'll see her in the morning."

"But she didn't even say goodnight," the little voice whined.

"Kylie, she's exhausted. You'll see her tomorrow." But the girl wasn't placated. Kristen could hear her whimpering through the door even as he finished his sentence.

Kristen wasn't the only one exhausted. Mark ran a hand through his thick hair as he watched his youngest daughter's light blue eyes fill with tears. Her little chin began to tremble and he knew he was in for a long night. Suddenly, he heard the door behind him open and out came Kristen.

"I'm sorry. We didn't mean to disturb you-"

She waved away the sentence. "It's okay."

She knelt down in front of their daughter, who immediately wrapped her small, chunky arms around Kristen's neck.

"I'm glad you're home, Mommy."

Kristen squeezed the tiny body close to her and whispered back, "I'm glad to be home too." She felt Mark's intense gaze on her and wondered if he could see through her lie. She pulled back and kissed the little girl on the head.

"Are you gonna be a good girl for your dad?"

Kylie nodded in acquiescence.

"Good. Then I'll see you tomorrow morning. Good night, sleep tight; don't let the bed bugs bite. Sweet dreams."

"Love you."

"Uh - love you, too." She smiled nervously and glanced at Mark. He gave her a look of mingled gratitude and sadness. He was grateful that she didn't break the poor kid's heart but he was sad because he knew she only said half the things she said to comfort the girl - not because she actually felt like a mother to their daughter. Kristen stood and nodded at Mark.

"Will you tell the other two I said goodnight?"

Mark nodded quickly. "Of course. Get some rest. And thank you." He looked like he wanted to say more than "thank you" but he restrained himself and Kristen didn't prompt him.

She smiled briefly before turning back into her room.

CHAPTER FOUR
Adjustment

Kristen woke up with a start. She'd had a restless night and was trying to put the pieces of her dream back together. A young man in a turban kept yelling at her in Pashtu.

"Get down! Get down!" he had yelled.

She didn't know how she understood him. But while she understood his words, she didn't understand the context or why she had dreamt it. It was the same dream she kept seeing every night since she'd woken up.

Lord, what are you trying to tell me? Are you trying to tell me something?

She sat up in the bed and glanced around her. Yesterday really had happened. She was in the strange man's home with his children - her children - *their children*. She shoved the dream aside. She had bigger things to worry about.

"Good morning, Dad!"

It was a little past seven in the morning but Mark was already up. By the time the kids came down to eat, he had already exercised, showered, read his devotional, packed their lunches, and cooked their breakfast. The girls entered the kitchen dining room with a bounce in their steps. They were grinning wildly and Mark knew it was because of their mom. He too couldn't stop grinning. When he'd woken up three hours earlier, he had cracked open her door to find her sleeping, just to confirm that the previous day really had happened. That she really was alive.

His son didn't look as happy; almost the opposite, in fact. He was quiet and wore a perpetual scowl as he ate his food. The more his sisters talked about Kristen, the more agitated he grew.

"Can you please stop talking about it?"

"About what?" Kylie asked, her spoon paused at her mouth.

"That woman."

"What did you just call her?" All three heads whipped towards their father in the kitchen. He looked down at his son with firm, almost fiery eyes, daring his son to repeat those words.

"Dad -"

"Caleb, I know this is difficult for you but I don't care how long it takes her to remember. You are never to address her as anything but 'Mom.' Is that clear?"

Caleb held his father's eyes silently, slightly longer than necessary. He nodded but made it clear in his expression that he didn't agree with his father's assertion. He asked the hard questions.

"So, what's gonna happen now?"

"I don't know. We're going to see a doctor today and figure out the next steps."

"What if she never remembers us?"

"We don't know if that will happen."

"But what if it does?" Caleb wouldn't let up. Mark touched his son's shoulder. He knew he was being obstinate and pessimistic on purpose but he also knew his son was hurting.

"Then we'll help build new memories."

"She's still our mom, Caleb." Jasmine said softly.

"Whatever." Caleb stood, jerking out from under Mark's hand. He grabbed his breakfast and went into the formal living room, a clear signal that he wanted to be left alone. Mark sighed. As grateful and happy as he was to have Kristen back, he knew this meant an uphill battle for his son.

Almost as soon as Caleb left the room, Kristen walked in.

"Good morning," she smiled nervously. Mark's face immediately lit up at the sight of her. The girls both gave her a hug and a warm greeting.

"You hungry?" he asked. He pointed to the stove. "I made you a plate."

"Thank you." She avoided his eyes once more. Every time she met them, it felt as if she were looking at the sun. The intensity was too much for her. If he noticed, he didn't act like it. He glanced at his watch.

"I've got to get them to school. Your doctor's appointment is at 9:00 so we'll go as soon as I get back, okay?"

She nodded, unsure of what to say. He smiled again, trying to put her at ease.

"Okay, kids, let's go."

Jasmine hugged Kristen goodbye and headed to the car but Kylie stayed wrapped around Kristen's leg and made it clear she didn't want to let go. Kristen smiled down at the chubby little girl. Her baby fat was fading but she was still adorable to watch and she endeared herself to Kristen by simply loving her. Mark had to remind her:

"Kylie, you'll see her again this afternoon. It's okay."

He gently coaxed Kylie off his wife's leg and led her to the garage. He was surprised to find his son already sitting in the car. He must have walked right past his mother in the midst of Kylie's separation anxiety. He glanced at his watch again. There wasn't enough time to confront him and make him greet his mother. He decided to let it go for the moment. Turning back, he saw Kristen watching him.

"I'll be back soon. Will you be okay here?" he asked in concern.

She nodded. He smiled once more and left.

"Mrs. Tyverson, it appears that you have suffered from a more severe case of retrograde amnesia," Dr. Ranja Sharma, the state's top neurologist, concluded. Mark and Kristen sat in her office as she pointed to the x-rays of Kristen's brain.

"We can't know exactly what happened because of the circumstances surrounding your accident but it appears that while you survived the bomb, you were close enough to the explosion to incur a diffuse axonal injury."

"What does that mean?" Mark asked.

"It's essentially structural damage to the brain caused by an external force."

"A brain injury?" Kristen asked.

"Correct."

"I'm brain damaged?"

The neurologist gave a gentle smile. "Not in the traditional sense of the term, Mrs. Tyverson." Kristen couldn't help but feel strange at the doctor's use of her married name.

Dr. Sharma continued, "Your motor and speech skills remain unimpaired. The coma gave your brain the time it needed to heal some of the more essential functions. That being said, the temporal lobe has been injured and this is what has triggered your memory loss. The good thing is this is retrograde amnesia and not anterograde amnesia - which would be the inability to create and maintain new memories."

"Jesus," Kristen muttered.

"Exactly," the doctor agreed.

"Will she be able to gain her memory back?" Mark asked.

"There is a chance that she will remember her past. Unfortunately, memory loss has no specific formula for recovery. Most patients regain some memories as time passes but there is no guarantee of recovery and even if that occurs, there is a chance that it will only be a partial recovery."

"Is there anything we can do to try and spur the memories back?"

The neurologist began shaking her head even before he finished the question.

"This sort of memory loss cannot be treated by the reminder effect, re-exposure to past events or personal information. You can try to re-orient her to her environment by familiarizing her with her current life but it won't trigger memories. That normally happens through spontaneous recovery."

"So it will either come back or it won't?" Kristen asked.

"Correct."

There wasn't much to discuss after learning the extent of Kristen's injuries. Dr. Sharma referred them to a physical therapist who could help with some of the after effects of her physical injuries. Mark managed to get a same day appointment and took Kristen straight to their office. A friendly young man of mixed heritage, in his late-twenties, Jack Vickson immediately put Kristen at ease.

"Why don't you go ahead and tell me your most immediate injuries."

"Besides my brain damage, you mean." Kristen smirked. Mark smiled sadly. "I have balance issues. I keep knocking into things by accident."

Mark had noticed her issues with balance when she first arrived the day before but he'd kept it to himself, not wanting to put her in even more discomfort.

She continued, "My right leg hurts a lot. If I stand or walk for an extended period of time, it'll start to tingle. My right knee sometimes buckles for no reason." This, he did not know and he turned to her in surprise.

Jack nodded. "The balance issue could be a result of your head trauma but it might improve when you feel steadier on *both* feet. Any other issues?"

"My head," Kristen said. "I...I get a lot of headaches. Ringing headaches."

Mark watched her in amazement. From all appearances, she seemed perfectly healthy and recovered but she was still enduring a great deal of discomfort. He felt a burning in his chest and kept quiet as she detailed her injuries.

"Do they come on their own or are they triggered by anything in particular?" Jack asked.

"I think they're triggered. Whenever I have a bad dream, I'll wake up with them." Kristen frowned. "When I'm awake, I'll get them whenever I'm stressed or overwhelmed."

Mark nodded even though she wasn't speaking to him. That was all he needed to hear as far as he was concerned. He would make it his goal to keep her as relaxed as possible to avoid any more headaches. He would take her to this therapist as often as possible to relieve her pain and get her stronger again. He was resolved.

Jack seemed resolved as well. He used the x-rays couriered from Reed and immediately put Kristen through a series of tests so that he could better gauge the extent of her injuries. Once he completed his chart, he had her do a couple exercises to relieve some of the tension in her joints and begin strengthening her weak spots. The center was a wholeness center fit with several departments, including a chiropractic practice. Jack teamed Kristen up with Dr. Laura Vosier, a blonde woman in her mid-forties and she made several adjustments to Kristen's spine, hips, collar bone, and extremities.

The whole appointment took close to two hours but it was worth it to Kristen. Her body felt ten times more relaxed and fluid than it had before. Areas she hadn't even known were out of place felt much better once they were in place.

Mark and Kristen settled in the car.

They both sat still for a few moments and neither said a word.

What happens next? Kristen wondered. She glanced at him and saw a stiff, determined set in his jaw.

"I'll pay you back," Kristen murmured. His head immediately snapped towards her.

"What?" He frowned.

"I'll pay you back," she repeated. "Are you upset about the costs? I'll cover it as soon as I'm working again."

He immediately put a hand up and looked at her in astonishment.

"You think I'm mad at you because of a co-pay?" The look he gave her immediately made her feel like an idiot for even thinking such a thing.

"Well, you're obviously upset about something. Is it the amount of time the appointments took? Did I make you late for something else? I know I'm being a drag so if this is disrupting things for you, just let me know and I'll ask Dierdra to-"

"Stop it," he said firmly. He looked even more upset than he had before. He gave her a searing look and said in no uncertain terms:

"I am your husband. You are my wife. Anything that is mine: money, time, resources, *anything* - is also yours. Kristen, I'm not upset about the appointments or the co-pay. I'm upset that you're in pain."

Understanding and surprise washed over her.

"I'm upset that your leg gives you trouble and that you get mind-numbing headaches. I'm upset that you were injured and that you're suffering as a result of it. At no point, and in no way, am I upset with *you*."

Kristen lowered her head, humbled and awestruck. He reached out and lifted her chin. When she met his eyes, they had an even deeper look of intensity than anything she had seen before. He spoke again, fervently.

"I want you to know that I will not rest until you are recovered. I will take you to as many neurologists, physical therapists, and chiropractors as it takes to make you feel completely well again. And whether or not you remember, I will do everything in my power to see that you are comfortable in our home and with our children."

His quiet declaration astounded her.

All she could think to say was, "Your family has been great."

He shook his head. "It's not my family, Kristen. It's *our* family. It always has been and it always will be."

She nodded and looked back down.

Mark watched her again and finally asked, "How are you feeling right now? Any headaches? Sore joints?"

She shook her head. "The anti-inflammatory stuff is kicking in. I'm okay."

"Would you be up for it if we took a walk together in the park?" She frowned in confusion. "Just a quick walk in the park. If you get tired at any point, we'll go straight home."

She looked at this man, whom she had only met a day ago and felt no reason to distrust him. She nodded her acquiescence and off they went.

The walk was awkward at first. Mark tried his best to get his wife to talk but she limited her responses to one word answers and soundless nods. He'd never seen her so quiet in all their years together, even when he first took her out. Finally, he said just as much and watched her squirm under his gaze.

"I'm sorry," she said quietly. "I'm just really struggling here."

She lifted her eyes to meet his and only saw understanding and patience in them.

"Do you have any questions about us? About our life together?"

They circled the pond at the center of the park, lush grass and green trees surrounded them along the pathway.

"Did we even have a good marriage?" she asked.

His gaze softened as he eyed her intimately. If she were white, she'd probably be red from head to foot.

"We've had a *great* marriage." *We still can*, he thought but didn't voice it as they made a turn around the pond. Kristen kicked at the leaves near her feet.

"I don't know how this happened. I'm not even into white guys."

He chuckled.

"Well, it looks like you changed your mind," he said humorously. "I met you when you were twenty-six. You were at *Rosetta*, celebrating an award you received with KJLH and I pulled you aside."

"Was I with other people?" she asked, her curiosity piqued.

"Your friends and your mom."

She was impressed. It took a lot of courage to approach a woman when surrounded by others. She voiced the same.

"I was nervous as hell," he admitted. "But I knew I would regret it if I didn't get your number. Seven months later, we were married." She heard a catch in his voice but when she looked up, his calm demeanor was still there.

"And I've already bore your children?"

He smiled at the way she said it. "Yes, you have given birth to two of my children. We adopted Jasmine a year after we got married."

"At least I don't remember the pain of childbirth."

He smiled wryly. "I see you still have your sense of humor."

She smiled back at him.

"What do you do?" she asked.

"I'm an accountant. I work out of our home and specialize in tax returns."

"What a boring profession," she blurted out before slapping her hand over her mouth and closing her eyes in humiliation. He laughed immediately and pulled her hand down.

"Sorry, I didn't mean to-"

"You act like you haven't told me this already." He rubbed the back of her hand as though trying to rub away the chagrined expression on her face. "I know it's not the most riveting profession but it's stable. I like numbers and I like stability. For me, it's the perfect fit."

She smiled up at him. She could see him as someone who enjoyed stability and practicality.

"But why did you marry a journalist? If my position has gone international, isn't there a lot of traveling and movement involved?"

He nodded like he had anticipated the question.

"When you first got the offer for ABC, we talked about this at length. You had already begun traveling a lot for your national seat and we knew it would only get worse. We decided to take the job and initially moved out to New York for it."

"We lived in New York?"

"For a time. But the strain of the job and the location wasn't a good fit for us. So you decided to leave the show."

"I did what?!" she asked in horror. He laughed again and explained:

"You decided to leave the show in order for us to move back to Atlanta and be close to our loved ones."

"Then how am I still an anchor with them?"

"I'm getting there, hold on." He looked down at her and smiled. This was the Kristen he knew and loved. The woman who could fire off questions like a battalion at war. She always thought ahead.

"They initially tried to replace you but you were so popular with viewers, their ratings took a serious dive when you left. ABC begged you to come back and offered to accommodate you by shooting the majority of the studio work in a rented facility in town. You still fly out to New York once a week to meet with the staff and there's still traveling for international specials, but it worked better than the New York move."

Kristen nodded, happy that she hadn't lost the job but nervous for what might be expected of her if she was *that* popular with viewers. She didn't even know if she still *had* a job. How did that work when you're presumed dead for a while and then return with severe amnesia?

"You're worried," Mark observed. He still held her hand and Kristen knew it was an invitation to share her thoughts and concerns but she felt tongue-tied. She still couldn't believe she married a white man and though she knew she needed to get over it, she didn't know how to when she wasn't familiar with *this* man in particular. She thought of all the times she felt uncomfortable in a white man's presence. By and large, she perceived them to be arrogant and condescending, though she knew that was a stereotype she had assigned to them and needed to overcome.

He led them to a bench facing the pond and sat down. When she settled next to him, he turned to her and asked her, hand still in his own:

"Is the fact that I'm white still throwing you off?"

Whoa! What was he, a mind reader? Kristen decided to be honest.

"Yes."

"Why?" He was a straight shooter.

"Because I can't imagine you *getting it*."

"About race, you mean?"

She nodded.

"Tell me what you're thinking."

She sighed and tried to pull her hand out of his but he held onto her.

"It's okay, Kristen. You can be straight with me."

She raised an eyebrow at him, almost impressed.

"Okay, what I'm thinking is, how on earth could I have married someone who I probably don't have a thing in common with? How could I have married a man who has never experienced being followed around in a store, pulled over for no reason, or passed over for work because of the color of his skin? How can I possibly relate to someone who has no idea what it's like to walk in the skin I'm in? And who do I talk to when things happen in relation to my race? You?"

"Absolutely."

"Absolutely *not*."

He raised a surprised eyebrow at her emphatic response.

"When two people marry, they are supposed to be able to share *everything* with each other. From my experience, people in the majority -"

"As in white people," he called her out.

At this, she yanked her hand out of his and stood up. He almost panicked, thinking she was done with the conversation when they were just making progress but she didn't leave; only began to pace in front of him.

"Yes, white people, don't want to acknowledge racial issues. It's either 'get over it' or 'I don't see race - I'm colorblind.' I'm sorry, but neither works for me."

"Nor does it work for me."

At this, she stopped pacing and faced him. Mark enjoyed the moment for what it was worth. For once, she was meeting his eyes without any hesitation or nervousness, too distracted by the subject matter to be self-conscious around him.

"Kristen, I don't pretend to be an expert on race relations and I know I'll never know what it's like to be a person of color but I do know a few things. I get that racism still exists and I get that it's an important issue. I understand that I have certain privileges as a result of being a white male that happens to be a result of historical and systemic injustices perpetuated in a societal cycle that I didn't even contribute to but benefit from."

Kristen's eyebrows shot up in surprise but Mark continued.

"In the same way it pisses you off that white people claim that beneficiaries of affirmative action don't deserve it, it bothers me when people assume I don't work hard for my career, assets and lifestyle. I know that our children will face prejudices and biases that I never will because they're darker than me. I know that you have faced your own share of ignorant people for no other reason than the shade of your skin. Does that qualify as '*getting it*'?"

She was astounded. She couldn't believe that he actually understood where she was coming from and was willing to lay out his stance in such an honest manner. All of a sudden it didn't seem so farfetched that she had married him. Mark raised an eyebrow at her mollified expression. She slowly sat back down and looked out at the pond as he watched her.

She eventually spoke, "What do you want from me?"

His voice softened at her bewildered expression. "I want to be your friend. I want to be your confidant. I want to be your lover." She looked at him sharply. "I'm being honest here. In no way will I force myself on you or push you before you're ready but I want to be your husband. Completely."

She looked down again.

"Kristen, you can trust me. I love you. That isn't going to change."

She took a deep breath. It was the first time she had heard him articulate it, although his actions had been nothing short of a loving husband.

"You don't know me," she replied but couldn't quite meet his eyes. She was afraid of what she might find if she looked at him, feelings so strong she couldn't even begin to return. She liked him but he was still a stranger to her.

"Yes, I do." he countered. "You don't know *me*. You can't love me yet because you don't remember. But I know you and I love you. And I hope you will get to know me again and possibly grow to love me. Just give me a chance. We'll take this one day at a time."

At this, Kristen did look up and saw a pleading look in his eyes. He had hope and he wasn't about to give up on her or the family they shared. Who was she to stop him?

"Okay."

When they left the park, they grabbed a quick lunch and headed home before the kids got back. Mark insisted that Kristen get some rest. She took a long nap while he got some work done. In what seemed like no time, the kids returned and were eager to see their mother - all except Caleb. Kristen had just woken up when they arrived and, feeling more refreshed, she sat with them in the kitchen's dining room and decided to kill two birds with one stone: get to know them and also catch up.

"Okay, so tell me some things I've missed."

Jasmine and Kylie immediately perked up. Caleb on the other hand, raised his eyebrows dubiously and looked back down at his plate of apple slices as though that challenge was impossible to meet. Mark watched him for a moment but chose to put his son's burgeoning attitude on the back burner. Again.

"I'll start," Jasmine said. "What's a big one? Kanye West and Kim Kardashian."

Mark frowned. "Really?"

"Who?"

Jasmine's mouth dropped. "Oh my God. You're unaffected by the Kartrashians. You are not caught up in the hurricane that is the overexposure of the Kardashian family."

"Wait a minute," Kristen frowned. "Are you referring to Robert Kardashian's family? The attorney that represented O.J. Simpson?"

"That's them," Mark answered. "Except, they are no longer known for Robert Kardashian's reputation but his middle daughter's exploits. He actually died in 2003."

"From what?"

"Esophageal cancer."

Jasmine added, "Then his daughter, Kim, made a se-"

"An inappropriate tape," Mark censored for Caleb and Kylie's sake. "And she became famous for no legitimate reason."

He could tell she was already getting bored with that subject. He turned to his daughters. "Tell her about the president."

"Holy-"

"Jasmine!" Mark warned.

"Sorry. Mom, we have a black president."

"What?!" Kristen exclaimed.

Mark smiled. Jasmine and Kylie nodded ecstatically.

"Who?" she asked.

"Barack Obama."

"Senator Obama? The Illinois state senator?"

"He's no longer a state senator," Mark replied. Kristen looked at him slightly longer than necessary and he knew she was wondering what his political affiliation was. He smiled again. They would address all that later.

Jasmine piped up, "We also have a black Disney princess-"

"No way!" Kristen gasped as her entire face lit up. She looked more excited about the princess than the President. Kylie ran over to the living room and retrieved *The Princess and the Frog* DVD case. She handed it to her mother and watched as she quickly scanned the premise described on the back.

They went on to try and tell her the biggest changes: the 2008 recession, Osama Bin Laden's death, the recent rash of school shootings, Prince William's marriage and child, Steve Jobs' death, Brad and Angelina's brood, Oprah's new network as well as the end of her show, and on and on it went. By the time the kids felt they had hit all of the important events, Kristen was stunned.

"Wow." She sat back in wonder and looked off pensively. Mark reached out and took one of her hands.

"How you doing?" he asked in concern.

She simply shook her head and continued to stare off. He glanced at his watch and announced: "Okay, kids, it's time for homework."

The girls immediately groaned in reluctance but Caleb was already pulling out his worksheets. Mark decided not to put it off any longer.

He turned to Kristen and said, "I'm going to talk to Caleb for a little. The girls will be busy with homework. Do you want to rest some more?"

She shook her head. "I'm going to call Dede and see what she's up to." He was nodding before she even finished her sentence. He could tell she was overwhelmed again and needed a familiar presence.

"How's your head?" he asked.

"Messed up," she replied. He looked at her. When she realized he was referring to her headaches, she quickly amended with, "I'm okay. Nothing hurts yet."

He smiled and nodded, taking hold of his son's shoulders and urging him out to the deck. Kristen watched them for a moment before heading back up to her room and grabbing the cordless phone. She dialed the number Mark had written for her and within two rings, Dierdra's voice yelled across the line.

"What's wrong? Is she okay? I've been calling all morning and-"

"Dee, it's me."

"Oh, thank God! *Where* have you been?" she exclaimed in a mellow-dramatic tone. Kristen rolled her eyes. Some things never changed.

"I was at the doctor's…several doctors, actually."

"They checked your head?"

"Yeah."

"And?"

"And…my memory will either come back on its own or it won't."

The other end was silent for a couple moments. Kristen could hear her take a deep breath.

"Okay. Okay, we'll get through this. The important thing is you're alive."

"Yeah," Kristen murmured. She was still struggling with that. Wondering if it really was a good thing that she had survived. She knew it was ungrateful and messed up of her but she couldn't help but wonder why she hadn't just died with all of her memories intact. She survived but she came home to a place that was not her home…to a life that was not her life…to a state of mind that was not accurate at all.

"I get off of work in thirty minutes," Dede said. An attorney-at-law, Dierdra's work revolved around billable hours.

"Can I come over?" It was as if she knew something was up.

Kristen nodded, even though she knew Dede couldn't see her.

"Yeah, I'd really like that." she said.

Mark sat next to Caleb on the steps of the wooden deck. He looked at the top of his head. Curly wisps of thick golden hair caught the sun and gave his son a halo effect. Caleb wouldn't look at his dad. He kept his eyes fixed on the large oak tree that held the family tree house.

Mark began. "How are you feeling about all this?"

Caleb shrugged. His eyes remained fixed on the tree. He wasn't going to crack that easily.

"Are you happy to see your mom back?"

"That's not her," he mumbled, almost incoherently.

Mark frowned. "What do you mean?"

"That's not Mom."

Mark waited.

"She looks like Mom and she sounds like Mom but she doesn't act like Mom. She's different."

"She doesn't remember."

Caleb shrugged.

"Do you blame her for not remembering?"

He shrugged again.

"I saw you when she first came back. You were happy to see her. You were right there with the girls, hugging her."

"She didn't hug us back." Mark's heart broke just a tiny bit at his son's quiet words.

"She loves you."

"No, she doesn't. She doesn't remember us."

"She wants to. She can't control it."

"*Fine!*" his son exclaimed. He kept his eyes on the tree but his face held an exasperated look.

Mark didn't know what to say. He'd never seen his son so upset and so closed off. He didn't know how to explain that while she didn't love them, it wasn't because Kristen was a malicious person. How can you expect anyone to love you when they don't know you? But how could he explain that to a nine-year-old child who did remember his mother loving him? Mark suddenly realized that his children, particularly his son, needed just as much attention and care as their mother did. He regretted all of the moments he had allowed to pass as he watched his son withdraw further and further away from the family unit. He rubbed the back of his neck and looked down at their feet. His large right foot settled next to his son's miniature left one.

"I love you, Caleb." It wasn't a planned response but it welled up inside his heart and poured out freely. For the first time since they sat out there, Caleb looked up at his father, his butterscotch cheeks filling with color. Mark met his son's eyes, the same brown as his own.

"I love you with all of my heart. I love you so much that I would die for you. You are my son and I don't ever want you to think that I don't love you." He saw the telltale signs of tears as his son's chin began to tremble and his eyes became slightly glassy.

"You don't understand it now and I'm sorry that all of this is happening but I want you to know that your mother's love is real. She loves you. Even though she doesn't remember you, deep down, in her soul, she loves you. I love you. Your sisters love you. And above all else, God loves you. No matter what happens or who changes, *you are loved*. Don't ever forget that."

The tears had long since spilled over and Mark wrapped a strong arm around his son's small frame, bringing him in for a long, warm embrace. He felt his son's little body shake as the tears worked their way out. Caleb tried to stifle the crying sounds but his father spoke to him gently, rubbing his back and assuring him:

"It's okay. Let it out. It's okay."

After a few minutes passed and the tears began to dry, Caleb pulled back slightly and looked up at his dad.

"I don't *have* to talk to her, do I?"

Mark was disappointed but he couldn't expect his son to do a full one-eighty in the course of a few minutes.

"Be nice. I don't want your mother to feel like a stranger in her own home. So be nice, okay?"

His son nodded. Mark gave him one last hug and watched him get up and head back into the house for his homework. He let out a sigh he hadn't realized he'd been holding.

"I wish I didn't come back."

There. She'd said it. Dierdra gave Kristen a slightly confused look before realization dawned on her.

"You don't mean that."

Kristen nodded. "Yes, I do. I wish I didn't come back. I wish I had just - I had just - di-"

"Stop it, Kristen!" Dierdra snapped. Kristen got off of the bed they'd both been sitting on and walked over to her room's window, overlooking the backyard. She watched as Mark stood up and headed back into the kitchen from the deck.

"You don't understand," she whispered.

She was beginning to think it was a bad idea inviting Dierdra over. Since her arrival, all she did was counter Kristen's concerns with empty promises of improvement and lukewarm reminders of Kristen's blessings.

Dierdra sighed. "You're right. I don't understand - not fully. And I'm sorry that I'm causing you more distress than comfort. But Kristen, I will not allow you to think along the lines of despair. 'The joy of the Lord is your strength.'"

Kristen whipped around. "Don't do that, Dee. Don't Bible-thump me. Doesn't Ecclesiastes say 'there is a time to weep and a time to laugh; a time to mourn and a time to dance'? For God's sake, Job's friends sat with him for three days in mourning and didn't say a word."

Dierdra looked slightly contrite. "I'm sorry. I get your point but keep in mind that Job lost all ten of his children, all of his wealth, and he and his wife were afflicted with sores. The only thing you've lost is your memory."

Kristen looked at Dierdra as if she'd just slapped her. Dierdra saw the look on her face and immediately regretted her words. She quickly tried to rectify it.

"Krissy-"

"I lost my mother, too."

"Kristen-"

"I know it's old news to you but it feels pretty fresh to me!"

"I'm sorr-"

"I think you should go."

"Let me explain."

"You've already said enough." Kristen walked into her adjoining bathroom and quickly locked Dierdra out. Her next words came through the door. "Thank you for coming, I'm sorry I've wasted your time."

Dierdra sighed again. She contemplated trying to cajole Kristen out of that bathroom but could tell from the determined look on her face that it wasn't going to happen. Kristen had already decided.

They were done talking for the day.

Dee walked up to the door and laid a gentle hand on it.

"I'll check in with you in a couple days. I love you, Kristen."

No response.

Inside, Kristen sat at the edge of the tub and lowered her chest to her knees. The medicine she'd had earlier was beginning to wear off; not only was she hurt by Dierdra's lack of understanding, her physical state was beginning to add to her pain. She heard her friend quietly exit the room and let out a sigh of relief. She hadn't expected the visit to go so wrong. If she couldn't get along with her best friend, the only person she remembered - how on earth was she supposed to adjust to her life with anyone else around? The sadness she had felt earlier began to grow and double in size. It permeated the room and choked her sense of peace.

Suddenly, she heard a light knock on the door.

"Kristen?" Mark called out.

She couldn't explain it but immediately, Kristen felt a sense of tranquility at the sound of her husband's voice. She uncurled herself from the tub and unlocked the door, cracking it slightly open. He looked down at his wife, his eyes sweeping over her with concern.

"Are you okay?" he asked softly. She shrugged. For a second, it reminded him of their son's response.

He asked, "What happened?"

Kristen opened the door and walked over to the bed. She sat down and watched as Mark towered over her, unsure of where he should go. She patted the bed in invitation. Relief washed over his face as he took a seat and waited for her to explain.

"What did Dede tell you?" she asked.

"It doesn't matter what she told me. I want to know what happened for you."

Kristen smiled then frowned. How could she tell him what happened from her perspective without hurting his feelings? She literally just told her best friend that she wished she hadn't returned home. She couldn't repeat that to Mark, could she?

Mark could read her face like no other.

"Don't worry about my feelings." He continued at her astounded expression, "You need to tell *someone* how you're feeling and if it's not Dierdra and it's not a therapist, then go ahead and tell me."

Kristen looked at him for a couple of moments. He looked as if he could face anything - any challenge she gave him.

"I told Dierdra I wish I hadn't come back."

Mark blinked. He hadn't expected her to be so blunt but he'd asked for it. He nodded slowly and waited for her to continue. Seeing that he hadn't overreacted to her statement or even rebuked her for it, Kristen continued.

"It's not that I don't like you guys. You all have been perfectly nice to me…well, almost all of you."

He smiled sadly at her. He'd wanted to tell her about his talk with Caleb but didn't know if she could handle it. It no longer felt like the right time to bring it up.

"I just feel too overwhelmed. I wish I had either come back with all of my memories intact or that I had just died. I'm upsetting you - maybe this was a bad idea."

She could tell Mark's emotions were straining under her words. He had a good poker face but his breathing was uneven and there was tension in his hands. Kristen began to stand up but instantly felt Mark's hand restrain her by the wrist.

"Don't," he said in a hoarse voice. "I'll be fine. I'm not going to lie. It hurts hearing you say this but I'd rather you tell me than hold it all in and not tell anyone. Why was it difficult to communicate this to Dierdra?"

"She wouldn't listen. She kept telling me that I shouldn't feel this way and that I should be grateful to be alive and to have all of the blessings I have."

"She always was a cup half-full kind of girl."

"Yeah. And I'm a pessimistic, ungrateful jerk." She put her hand up at his incoming protest. "No, I am. I know I shouldn't feel this way. I know I should just suck it up and make do but I don't even know *how*. I don't even know where to start. And quite frankly, I'm scared to go to sleep and I'm scared to wake up."

"Why?" Mark asked softly. He'd long since forgotten about keeping his expression in check and Kristen could see how deeply this was hurting him. The sight made her eyes begin to water.

"When I go to sleep, I get nightmares. When I wake up, there's no relief but a new anxiety. I don't know my place here. Where I belong. Who might I offend today? When is the job situation going to be resolved? How do I spend my time without bothering other people...?" she tapered off in visible frustration.

He was beginning to feel overwhelmed just listening to her. *Lord, how do I help her? How do I get her to see that she belongs here? I need my wife. I can't lose her again.*

Then love her.

It was a still, small voice that answered unexpectedly. Mark wasn't the sort to say he heard God's voice regularly - he often used the Bible and prayer to make his decisions; but somehow he knew that simple answer hadn't been his own thought. He looked at his wife, her brown skin taut with worry and anxiety. She was still beautiful to behold, even in the midst of her stress. He loved her - whether she remembered him or not. Slowly, he wrapped an arm around her and pulled her to his chest. She stiffened at first but eventually released herself fully into his arms. He held her tightly and rocked her wordlessly.

It was what she needed all along.

"Do you want to rest a bit more? Relax?"

"You keep asking me that." Kristen smiled and shook her head. "I actually need to figure out my hair situation."

Mark cocked his head at her and smiled. He fixed his gaze on her small afro and noticed it was shorter than before, more brittle, and definitely in need of some attention.

"When did I go natural?" she asked.

"About eight years ago. You were tired of the 'creamy crack.'" Mark answered.

She chuckled at the nickname for chemical relaxers.

"Well, I have no idea what to do with it."

"I'll help you," he said easily.

She looked up at him and quirked a brow.

"What do *you* know about it?"

He smiled at the unspoken question. What would a white guy know about doing natural black hair?

"You'd be surprised how much I picked up as you went on your natural hair journey. Besides, who do you think does Kylie's hair now days?"

"Jasmine."

He laughed, stood up and left the room. Moments later, he returned, holding several jars, combs, and brushes. For the next hour, he explained the different products she liked to use, when, and for what. He showed her how to detangle and twist her ends and caught her up to speed on different hair care terms.

"So a co-wash is when you wash your hair but you only use a conditioner. You usually do this once or twice a week after you workout so that you don't dry your hair out."

She nodded and watched him closely. Never in a million years did she think she'd be learning how to take care of her hair from a white man. And yet, there was something endearing about him knowing so much about her routine, culture, and an integral part of her identity. Only someone in love would know so much about something otherwise insignificant to him.

"A wash and go is when you basically rinse your hair in the shower, towel dry it, and then let it air dry as you go on about your day...at least..." he held out his hands. "This is my understanding of it. Maybe Dierdra can give you more details."

"You're doing just fine." Kristen smiled. "So if I had permed hair when we first met, how did you feel about me doing the big chop and going natural?"

"I loved it," Mark said without hesitance. "You're beautiful no matter what you do. And I'm glad you're natural because now you don't freak out about going in the pool or having it rain and getting your hair wet. I love it. I love you."

He looked back down as color rose in his cheeks. She smiled and placed a hand over his. He looked back up at her.

"Thank you," she said softly.

CHAPTER FIVE
Understanding

Shortly after Mark and Kristen had their heart to heart, they came up with a plan of attack for Kristen's foray back into normal life. Though they tried, neither could have prepared for the whirlwind ahead of them. Mark contacted their personal attorney and their personal attorney contacted several authorities as well as ABC Headquarters to announce Kristen's return. After the shock of her survival passed, the buzzards descended.

In less than twenty four hours, a national investigation was opened and Kristen was questioned about the events surrounding her accident. Questions immediately arose as to how she was the only person to survive such a blast. Who was the mysterious man who saved her? Authorities quickly realized they would get nowhere with an amnesiac and requested an inquest to further investigate the tragedy at the actual site. Kristen quickly realized that her ordeal was more than just an incident that affected her and her family - it was a political, legal, and public matter to contend with.

The investigation had *just* shifted from Kristen when ABC decided to make public news of her survival and return. Overnight, she, Mark, and their family were swarmed with press inquiries. Their once quiet, humble abode transformed into a media frenzy so disconcerting, the local police had to intervene. Kristen felt as though she were out of body watching CNN, ABC, CBS, and MSNBC newscasters and pundits talk about the revelation of her survival and the discovery of her amnesia. She saw playback footage of the public memorial held in her honor and the numerous shrines built when the public thought she had passed. She saw clips of her work as an anchor, national and international, and sat astonished at the amount of news she had covered, dignitaries she had met, all of which she had no recollection. Even more astonishing was the outpour of congratulations and joy at the news of her return from all corners of the world. The studio at ABC was flooded with "get well soon" cards and all of the condolence letters Mark received were replaced with tokens of relief and gratitude at her survival. Numerous media outlets sought her out for an exclusive first interview. She and Mark opted to keep it simple and released a statement, briefly explaining her return, her amnesia, and thanking the public for their prayers and support.

Surprisingly, the easiest aspect of her return was the legality of it. In Georgia, there existed a statute that prevented any missing person to be declared dead in absentia until four years after their disappearance. An exception could have been made for a public figure like Kristen but Mark had been too grief-stricken to go through the paperwork. Now, it was unnecessary. Her passport, visas, and driver's license intact, Kristen could return to life as normal at least on paper.

She was eager to get back to the one thing she remembered doing: reporting. She had arranged for a meeting with several ABC *World News* producers at the headquarters in Manhattan and was surprised to find that they were eager to meet with her as well.

"Kristen, we're so glad you're back!" said a tall, middle-aged man as he warmly shook her hand.

"You must be Lance," Kristen replied cautiously. Mark had prepped her prior to her meeting, showing her photos of all the key players at the studio. She was pleased to find several of them waiting for her in the studio lobby.

But not a single face sparked her memory.

The tall man's smile saddened slightly but he welcomed her all the same.

"Yes, Lance Carson. I've been on the team since you first joined back in 2010." He stepped aside and pointed to a short Asian woman in her early thirties.

"This is Lila Chang, my co-producer. You two come up with many of the stories the show will do."

The two shook hands.

Lila's smile was genuine and wide. "Welcome back, Kristen."

"Thank you."

She was introduced to several other producers, writers, and executives who all seemed very happy to see her before they escorted her to a large, sleek boardroom.

Lance started without preamble.

"Kristen, I'm sure that you are still in the middle of adjusting to life back home. We wanted to lay out our cards on the table and let you know that your seat is still open to you if you want to take it."

Kristen's jaw dropped.

"You're serious?"

Lance nodded and so did the others in the room.

"Dead serious. We met with Dan Blonsky, the head of ABC, shortly after Mark notified me of your survival. If you're willing to have us, we want you back on the show as soon as possible."

"But didn't you hire a replacement anchor?"

He shook his head. "Not yet. You were three years into a seven year contract. We had a series of rotational anchors because the audience wasn't ready for a permanent host. In fact, we were beginning negotiations with a couple of candidates but then you returned."

"But what about my...you know...?"

Lila spoke up, "Kristen, we're not concerned about your memory loss. We want you to recover, of course, but it shouldn't affect your ability to report on current events so long as enough research is done ahead of time."

Kristen nodded. It was the same argument Mark had voiced when she had mentioned her concerns. She couldn't help but think of him back at the hotel. She had refused to allow him in the meeting with her, wanting to handle it on her own, but he had insisted on escorting her to New York, trusting Jasmine to babysit. Dierdra and Kristen had made up during the media whirlwind and she was tasked with checking in on the kids every few hours while they were away.

The perfect gentleman the entire trip, Mark had reserved one room with two beds. He was waiting in their room at that very moment. Kristen lowered her head and smiled, imagining the look on his face when she told him the news.

"Kristen?"

Her head popped back up and she saw the anxious expression of all those in the boardroom. She then realized she hadn't given her answer.

"There won't be any traveling anytime soon." Lance added. "We'll have other reporters support you in that area. All you have to do is shoot from the studio in Atlanta and meet with us here every other week."

They really were eager to have her back and because of that, she only had one question.

"When do I start?"

"How did it go?" Mark asked as soon as she walked into the room.

They were staying in a high rise hotel in the middle of the Upper East Side. Dark red rugs adorned the hardwood floor. The furniture consisted of ornately decorated dark wood fixtures and a small chandelier lit the entire room. Kristen looked around the room and still couldn't believe she and Mark could afford such a luxurious suite.

Middle-aged money, she thought. *Wow, this is nice.*

"Well?" Mark pushed. He knew she was admiring the suite but he was dying to know how it all went. He had been concerned that they would take advantage of her condition but he had to remind himself that Kristen had always been shrewd - even as a twenty-six-year-old.

She finally met Mark's eyes and smiled.

"I'm in."

She laughed as he leapt from the bed and caught her up in his arms. He gave a whoop of jubilation and spun her around in circles.

He stopped spinning and held her closely as he whispered in her ear, "Congratulations. I knew you could do it."

Her laughter died down at the feel of herself in his embrace. His arms felt like bands of steel that made her feel warm and safe. He'd been amazing the whole time; taking the press issues in stride, supporting her with her work situation, and still managing to take care of the kids single-handedly. He kept revealing his character to her in his actions and it made him all the more attractive to her. Her face was tucked in his shoulder and she could smell his fresh, masculine cologne. It made her feel lightheaded and a tension coiled in her lower belly that felt foreign to her. She couldn't recall making love to this man but all of a sudden, it was on the forefront of her mind.

She pulled back, slightly panicked, and whispered, "Thank you," without meeting his eyes.

She felt his hands fall down from around her and didn't have to look at him to know his disappointment and hurt.

"I'm sorry," Mark said quietly. "I didn't mean to make you feel-"

"It's not you, it's me. *I'm sorry.*" She turned away from him and sat on the edge of her bed. The large beautiful suite suddenly felt small as the tension rose between them. Mark sat beside her and gently grabbed her hand.

"You know that I've been seeing Dr. Longinow."

The shrink.

Kristen nodded. She knew where this was going but kept her silence.

"I really think she could help you - help *us* - get to a better place."

She closed her eyes and shook her head.

"I'm sorry. I can't. I…" How could she explain to him her reasons behind rejecting therapy? People saw therapists all the time - it had nothing to do with any antiquated stigma attached to it. Little did she know that Mark had expected that response. He knew exactly why she was refusing to go.

He nodded and squeezed her hand.

"I won't push you but I want you to keep an open mind and consider it."

She finally looked at her husband. "Okay."

He smiled. "So tell me more about the meeting. When do you start?"

She recounted the details of the meeting and how eager they were to have her on board.

"I start next week," she announced. Mark raised surprised eyebrows.

"You're okay with that?" he asked.

"Yeah," she nodded. "Are you?"

He looked off in contemplation for a moment, unconsciously folding his hands, but he quickly met her eyes again.

"Yes, I am. I think it'll help you to go back to doing what you love. And I think it'll help you feel more acclimated to the life you can't remember. As long as you aren't going overseas...?" he trailed off in a questioning tone.

She shook her head. "Nope. And I'm only meeting them here once every *two* weeks."

He smiled, surprised.

"Then, I don't see a problem with it. I'm proud of you," he finished warmly.

Kristen looked at him in wonder and shook her head.

"You are a very supportive husband, Mark Tyverson."

"I have a wonderful wife worth supporting, Kristen Tyverson."

Kristen felt heat rush to her face and was grateful he couldn't see her blush.

"Why did you choose me?" she asked suddenly.

He frowned in confusion before understanding dawned on him. And then he shook his head in wonder.

"I don't think I chose you. And I don't think you chose me. I think God did the choosing and we just followed along."

She grinned widely, surprised and delighted by his response.

"How long have you been a believer?" she asked.

"Since I was a teen. My family raised me in the church but I didn't accept Christ for myself until I was seventeen - right before college."

Kristen whistled. "You got caught right before you could go crazy."

He laughed. "I know. I had all these plans to get drunk and party at frat houses. And then He grabbed my heart…and I didn't want to do all that anymore."

She nodded, completely in sync with him. "I didn't take my faith seriously until I was sixteen. It totally blew my college plans but it was probably for the best."

He nodded with a mock frown, "I think so too."

They laughed.

"You studied accounting as an undergrad?" she asked.

He looked at her for a second. It pleased him that she was asking questions and he didn't mind that he had answered them years before. He was grateful that she was expressing any interest in him.

"No, actually. I was a biology major. I thought I wanted to practice medicine eventually but three years into my major, I realized I didn't want to sacrifice my family time for my career so I earned my Masters in Accounting and started my own practice."

Kristen shook her head.

"What?" he asked.

"Who thinks like that at twenty or twenty-one? When I was in school, all I could think about was how I wanted to kill it as a journalist. I never considered the adjustments I would have to make for a family. I thought I'd figure it out later."

She looked up at his profile and saw him blushing.

"I think it's very admirable," she added.

He met her eyes and she saw a look flash in them; one of longing and intense desire. The look was so unexpected, so raw, they both sat in the tension of it for a few moments, neither daring to make a noise. Finally, he tore his eyes away from hers and stood up. Keeping his back to her, he said in a hoarse voice:

"Our plane leaves in less than three hours." He cleared this throat. "We should probably start getting ready."

"Mark-"

He turned around, eyes blazing. "I'm not the enemy here. You know that, right, Kristen?"

She gasped. "Of course not. Why would you say that?"

"Why are you so withdrawn?" he countered. "Every time I touch you or get close to you or happen to look at you for longer than a second, you pull away. Why?"

"This still feels weird to me. You're-"

"I'm your husband."

They let that statement hang in the air. Mark closed his eyes and heard a familiar verse come to him immediately:

"Love is patient, love is kind. It does not envy, it does not boast, it is not proud. It is not rude, it is not self-seeking, it is not easily angered, it keeps no record of wrongs... bears all things, believes all things, hopes all things, endures all things. Love never fails."

It was a mixture of two different translations but the message was loud and clear. He was called to love Kristen and love her in a selfless way. Mark looked at his wife and for the first time saw the lone tear that ran down her cheek. Her shoulders hunched over she stared off into the New York City skyline and he immediately felt shame for his impatience.

This should be the highlight of her week and I just ruined it. Oh God, please help me turn this around.

Kristen felt a weight sink into the bed right next to her. She refused to look in his direction. All she could think about was how miserable she was making him.

What's wrong with me, Lord? Why won't you let me remember?

'In all things, God works for the good of those who love him.'

What does that mean? What good could come from this amnesia?

She felt Mark's large warm hand envelope hers and the touch gave her comfort.

"I'm sorry, Kristen."

She looked at Mark in confusion and then, as though just noticing the tear on her cheek, she swiped it away and said, "You didn't do anything wrong. I'm the one with the messed up head."

He shook his head and looked down at her face. She was so beautiful, he longed to kiss her but he looked back down at his hands and took a deep breath instead.

"It's not your fault that you don't remember me. And a part of not remembering me is not really knowing me or feeling comfortable around me. *I* need to remember that and be more patient. And I will."

"I want to remember you."

Mark's eyes snapped back to hers in surprise.

"You do?"

She nodded, tears back in her eyes.

"Do you think He'll ever let me remember?"

He knew who she was referring to.

"I don't know, Kristen. He works in mysterious ways. Whether He gives you your memory back or not, He's given you back to me. Back to our family. I can't fathom asking for anything better."

CHAPTER SIX
Passing Time

"Caleb! Get down here - we're gonna be late!"

It was another hectic morning in the Tyverson household and everyone had their part to play. Kristen had only been back at work for a couple of weeks and already the family had established a routine. Every morning, Mark woke up at 4:30 to do his devotional and exercise. To his surprise - and concern - Kristen was always out of the house before then. She went to the gym at the crack of dawn every morning and worked out for a good three hours. By the time she returned home, the kids were waking up and getting ready for school. She would do a quick devotional, hop in the shower, and dress for work.

She made her way to the stairs at the same time Caleb did.

"Good morning," she said, smiling nervously.

He looked up at her and quietly replied, "Good morning."

Though he was less hostile in her presence, he still hadn't quite warmed up to her and Kristen didn't know how to make it better. She watched the small boy retreat down the stairs with his backpack, almost as large as him, and found it hard to believe that he was her son - her child. The girls unwaveringly treated her like their mother even though she didn't feel very maternal but Caleb kept his distance and made it hard for her to fathom ever having carried him in her womb.

Kristen shook the thought away and joined everyone else in the kitchen. The girls greeted her with warm hugs. As always, Mark immediately lit up and greeted her as well.

"Good morning."

"Good morning."

His eyes roved over her tailored navy pantsuit before meeting her eyes. She looked self-conscious under his perusal and it didn't escape him that she kept fidgeting with her hair and suit jacket. His eyes told a thousand stories but he kept his words simple.

"You look beautiful," he said softly.

She smiled at him. "Thank you."

"What he means is you look 'hot' - don't you, Dad?" Jasmine teased her father.

He blushed and nodded, looking back down at the breakfast he was plating.

"Your mother is both," he surmised.

Jasmine smiled and winked at her mom as Kristen shot her a warning look. Mark placed Caleb's plate before him as he took a seat at the dining table then quickly handed Kristen hers.

"I told you, you don't have to do this for me," she reminded him.

He waved the sentence away.

"I want to. You've been working like crazy. The least I could do is save you time making breakfast."

When Kristen wasn't at the studio recording, she was in the library researching current events and trying to catch up on all she had missed. She still remembered the shock of finding out that all footage had switched from film to digital and that many of the tech positions crew members once held were now obsolete in light of technological advances, including a new device called ParkerVision. During her first day back, she had expected to find roughly ten to twelve people in the studio when in fact there were only three people - the director, the on-site producer and the technician handling the ParkerVision. On top of that, she had to learn about Facebook and Twitter, Instagram and YouTube - all important platforms that not only promoted her show but sometimes provided news stories. She shook her head and dug into the food.

He leaned against the counter and watched her take a bite of the omelet. She rolled her eyes back in sheer pleasure and he loved that she openly enjoyed his cooking. He wished they could both just stop and take time to become reacquainted but at their break neck pace, they were both two ships passing in the night.

"*You've* been working like crazy too," she said around her bites. "Isn't tax season the most stressful time for you?"

He ran a hand through his thick brown hair at the reminder. He had eighteen accounts that were due at the end of the week, seven of which had very complicated components to address. Like Kristen, he was working both weekends and nights and while he wasn't behind on his work, he wasn't far enough ahead to be anywhere near relaxed about it.

Kristen looked him over. He was tired, with small bags under his eyes, and a five-o-clock shadow covering his handsome jaw. His hair stood up in spiked frustration and his eyes held a constant look of concern. Dressed in a dark gray sweater with khaki cargo pants, his tall frame slouched against the counter as he rubbed the back of his neck unconsciously. Kristen felt an unexplainable surge of compassion for him; a desire to serve him somehow.

Lord, he's doing too much. How can I ease his workload?

The answer came to her immediately.

"I'll take the kids to school."

All four heads whipped around to face her in surprise. Mark frowned.

"You don't have to. I can do it-"

"No, I want to." Kristen insisted. "You've been handling everything on your own for too long. I know where the schools are and it's en route to the studio. I can take them."

Mark was shocked. Kristen had been back for almost a month and had never expressed an interest in taking the kids anywhere. He didn't blame her; she didn't feel like they were her kids but he couldn't help but feel relief at having some of the pressure taken off. Three straight months of acting like a single father had taken its toll on him.

He looked at her and smiled as she already began gathering the kids and escorting them to the garage door. He followed them to the exit and watched as the kids climbed into her sleek sedan, parked next to his. He held her back for a second while the kids fought over shot gun. She looked up at him with questioning eyes.

"Thank you," he said in low timbre.

She smiled and impulsively kissed his cheek.

"No problem."

Her eyes mirrored his surprised expression and she quickly strode to the car as if in shock from what she had just done. A small smile came to his lips as he watched her back out of their driveway.

You're melting her resolve, aren't you? he prayed. *Bring her back to me.*

The drive to Bartholomew Academy was a short one. Only ten minutes away from their neighborhood, Jasmine and Kylie managed to fill the ride with all of the current events in school. The girls were roughly ten years apart in age but got along like two peas in a pod. Kristen couldn't help but chuckle at their camaraderie. Caleb remained silent the entire drive, keeping his gaze fixed on the manicured streets and homes that passed by as they approached the private Christian school.

As soon as Kristen pulled the car to a stop, Caleb got out without a backward glance.

"What's wrong with him?" Kylie asked.

Jasmine shook her head and glanced at Kristen. "He's just being rude. Sorry, Mom."

Kristen shrugged, "It's okay."

They watched Caleb walk towards the building with his shoulders hunched forward. He didn't look eager to go in.

"Do you think it has to do with his grades?" Kylie asked.

"His grades?" Kristen looked between the two girls.

Jasmine shot Kylie an irritated glare.

"She wasn't supposed to mention it. Dad doesn't want you worrying about it."

"About what?" Kristen pushed. Now her curiosity was piqued.

"Well...Caleb has been having issues with his grades ever since he transferred into Ms. Walker's class this semester."

"Ms. Walker?"

"Yeah," Jasmine pointed out the window. "See that tall, blonde lady in the long pink dress?"

Kristen nodded.

"That's Ms. Walker. Caleb hasn't been doing so hot since transferring into her class. It's weird because Caleb has always been good in school. A straight-A student even before he started getting letter grades."

Kristen frowned. "What does Mar - your dad - think of this?"

Jasmine shrugged. "He thinks it's because of everything that's been going on."

Kristen looked at her eldest and knew she meant everything that had been going on with her accident and disappearance. Jasmine glanced at her and smiled.

"He hired Caleb a tutor and they've been meeting twice a week so hopefully that'll turn it around. Don't worry."

"Okay," she replied. "Well, you girls have a great day."

Jasmine turned to her and hugged her before hopping out. Kylie wrapped her arms around her from the back seat and jumped out as well. They both turned to the car and waved.

"Bye! Love you!" they cried.

"Love you, too!" Kristen replied

It wasn't until she was halfway to the studio that she realized how easy it was for her to say it that time around.

I really do love them, she thought.

How could she not?

The shoot that day was straightforward and easy. With the script already written, Kristen simply showed up at the studio, spoke briefly with the producer and director, sat in front of the camera and read the TelePrompTer on set. Several stories and several takes later, she was done for the day. As soon as the director called it a wrap, she stood to assemble her things and head over to her physical therapy appointment.

Jason Peterson, the producer, asked for a word.

"What's going on?" she asked.

"I know you're traveling back to New York for the meeting this coming week."

She nodded.

"Lance and I were talking. He wanted to know if you wanted to be featured on Carissa Perry's panel for the Friday night segment. Perry needs a strong panel to help the dipping ratings and you would be perfect for the spot."

"Is it live?" Kristen asked.

He nodded. "It is but you would be prepped on the topics beforehand and the segment itself is only about fifteen minutes. You would come on towards the end of the show and it'll be over before you know it."

"I don't know…"

"Lance wasn't sure you'd want to do it but he did reason that guest appearances always help our ratings for *World News* and you haven't done one since you've been back."

She was nodding before he finished his sentence.

"Okay, let's do it."

⁓

"Well, Kristen, it looks like you're showing a lot of improvement." Jack concluded.

Kristen agreed. It was hard to believe that only a month ago physical therapy had been a painful necessity in her life. But as she continued going to her daily appointments, Kristen felt noticeably stronger and actually looked forward to her sessions.

Jack had put her through several reps of strengthening exercises for her back and legs. He tested her balance and deemed her well enough to try her luck on a balance beam. Though she slipped a couple of times, she fared much better than either of them had expected. As a part of their cool down, Jack had her stretch out her hamstrings while he gauged her flexibility.

"So when will you give me the green light to stop coming?" Kristen asked.

Jack chuckled. "You're doing better but you're not quite there yet. Besides," he glanced at her with a mischievous grin, "what would I do if you left me already?"

"Find another helpless victim to torture."

"Aww, that's not fair. No pain no gain, right?" He looked at her with a charming smile. "You've done an incredible job, Kristen. I'm very proud of you."

Kristen smiled politely and looked down at her arms extended over her legs. It had only been a week since she had convinced Mark to stop taking her to all her appointments but in that time, Jack had begun to flirt with her unashamedly. She shrugged it off as him just teasing her.

I'm married with three kids and I have the stretch marks to prove it. Why would he be seriously flirting with me?

The thought made her very self-conscious in their private space. Her self-awareness had grown more and more since her return and it made her less and less satisfied with her physique. She was used to being slender and toned. She didn't know if it was her injury or her experience bearing children that had changed her body so drastically. She was a size six and had never been anything more than a size two. She went to the gym every day, seven days a week, in an attempt to shed the weight. Even more frustrating was the amount of time it was taking for her to lose it.

"When will I be able to do more cardio?" she asked. Jack had specifically warned her against overdoing it in the gym. She neglected to tell him how long she worked out and how often but she did follow his advice to avoid re-injuring herself.

Jack silently assessed her for a moment and then said, "Probably in another two weeks or so. I'll have to test your joint strength."

She nodded. "I'll hold you to it."

"I know you will."

Mark was knee-deep in his work by the time she returned.

"Holy guacamole." Kristen muttered to herself at the site of his office. Papers were strewn about his desk. He stood in front of a large white board that almost took up the entire wall space. The board itself was full of mathematical equations and notes she couldn't even begin to comprehend if she tried.

And she would never try.

At the sound of her voice, Mark immediately dropped the dry eraser in his hand and turned to her. He smiled, always happy to see her.

"Hey! How was your day?"

He took a step forward and then stopped himself. He didn't know how long it would take for him to remember that hugging and kissing her in greeting was still out of her comfort zone. Every time he saw her after a long day, he had to control his impulse to hold her. She smiled and looked away, very much aware of his last minute save.

She looked back up and pointed at the board.

"Just looking at that makes my head hurt. Have you been working on this all day?"

He grinned and shook his head. "Only for the past hour. I got through eight more clients today so that's good."

She pointed at the massive tax law book propped open on his desk.

"How often do you need to refer to that?"

"Every year. And every year, there's a new one to refer to. With 'Obamacare' in effect, there are a lot of laws I have to be mindful of."

Kristen nodded, still somewhat fuzzy on the logistics and impact the President's groundbreaking legislation had on everyday citizens. The mention of the new law once again piqued her curiosity about Mark's political views, but she put that thought on the back burner.

"So, do we do our taxes together or separately?" she asked. He raised his eyebrows.

"Oh, yeah, I don't know why I didn't mention it earlier. I do our taxes every year."

He reached into the metal filing cabinet next to the desk and retrieved a file Kristen saw labeled as "Fed/GA 2013 Return." He handed it to her and she perused the perfectly filed return.

"We should receive our refund in a couple of weeks."

Since her return to work, Kristen had learned that she and Mark shared their income for the most part. They had a joint checking and savings account but allocated a small amount of spending money for each to do with as they pleased without having to consult the other. Kristen thought it a smart plan. When she met with their banker, she had been floored to discover that she and her husband had shared assets valued in the millions. While a large chunk of that money came from her successful career on *World News*, Mark had contributed a sizeable fortune through his accounting firm, which she discovered represented well-known athletes, celebrities, and businesses in Atlanta. To put it simply, she and her husband were both killing it in their fields and were paid accordingly. She never would have guessed it from the way they lived, though. They were certainly affluent, with enough resources to send all of their children to private school, but they didn't lead extravagant lives of luxury. Much of their wealth went back out into charity and missionary work and she was glad.

Kristen returned the documents to him.

"How was work?" he asked.

"It was good. I've been invited to be a part of a panel on Carissa Perry's show."

He raised his eyebrows in surprise. "That's pretty huge. Are you going to do it?"

Kristen frowned. "Do you think I can do it?"

She was testing him.

"You can do anything," he replied without hesitation.

He passed.

She smiled. "I said yes."

He smiled. "Good. So how was the drive this morning?"

She nodded. "It was good. They all behaved."

He was watching her closely and she knew he was looking for nonverbal clues.

"Even Caleb?" he asked and Kristen quickly understood why he was so curious.

"Even Caleb. I mean…he didn't say anything the entire ride. I did learn something interesting though." She met her husband's eyes. "Jasmine told me about the situation with his teacher." She saw a frown darken his face.

"I told them not to worry you with that."

"Kylie let it slip by accident. But like I told Jasmine, I'm not worried. I'm just curious. Jasmine said he's always been a good student."

Mark placed a hand at the nape of his neck and rubbed up and down. Kristen noticed that he did that whenever he was uneasy about something.

"Yeah, he has. I think it's just a result of everything that's happened. He's had so many changes. I hired a tutor to help him during the weekend and some evenings."

"Has it helped?" Kristen asked.

Mark shrugged. "Slightly. His multiple choice assignments are always perfect. It's his essays that get the lower grades. I'm keeping an eye on it."

Kristen nodded. She looked around the room awkwardly and tried to figure out the best way to excuse herself. Mark looked down at her and could see that she was anxious to leave. He wished he could make her feel more relaxed around him but he reminded himself to be patient.

"Hey," he said softly. She looked up again. "The kids and I are going back to church this Sunday. Will you join us?"

For the first time in a while, Kristen felt excited. She grinned and simply said:

"It's about time."

2 Hours Later:

"Guess what I have?" Kylie asked in a sing-song voice. She pulled the purple box from behind her back.

"Samoas!" Kristen exclaimed. She and Jasmine dove right into the package and immediately enjoyed the coconut, chocolaty delight. The three girls chatted about Jasmine's day as Kylie gave her blunt, uninvited opinion on all of her older sister's friends. Kristen sat back and laughed as her daughters bickered over the trustworthiness of one of Jasmine's closest friends. She didn't laugh for long though. A few minutes into the conversation, Kristen began to hold her stomach and her head.

"Mom?" Jasmine noticed first. "Mom, are you okay?"

Kristen shook her head. "My stomach...my *head*."

It wasn't the same headache she was used to but a different kind that started and stayed on the front left side of her skull. She leaned forward in her seat and took deep breaths as Jasmine got up and sought her dad.

Seconds later, Mark emerged and immediately knelt by Kristen's side. He rubbed her back in the soothing circles she had grown used to and asked her calmly, "What's wrong?"

"My stomach feels unsettled. It keeps churning and it hurts. My head hurts too but it's not the same as it usually is."

"She was fine just a minute ago."

"Did she eat anything?"

"Hello? I'm right here," Kristen reminded them.

Mark smiled. "Sorry. Did you eat anything just now?"

"Just those cookies. I love Samoas."

Mark glanced at the emptied box as understanding dawned on him. He looked at Jasmine and could see when she caught on herself.

"Oh, I totally forgot," she said. "Sorry, Dad."

He shook his head, "It's okay. It's not your fault." He turned to Kristen. "Your body is reacting to the gluten in the cookies. You have Celiac disease."

Kristen looked at him as though he grew horns right in front of her.

"What the hell is Celiac disease?"

"Yeah," Kylie repeated. "What the hell is Celiac disease?"

"Kylie!" Mark scolded her, "You are not to use that word again. Do you understand me?"

He turned back to see Kristen slap a hand against her forehead.

"I'm sorry, Mark. I didn't even think- "

"It's okay," he smiled at her reassuringly. He glanced at their youngest, who gave an impish grin. "She knows better."

He refocused his attention on her. "Celiac disease is a gluten intolerance."

"Gluten is…?"

He tried to explain it to the best of his ability and Jasmine mentioned the recent rise of people who were discovering gluten intolerances in their system.

"You just happen to be one of them."

"Great," Kristen frowned. "So I can't have cake or cereal or cookies or bread or anything that tastes remotely good."

Jasmine began to laugh at her mother's melodramatic assessment and Mark couldn't help but join in.

"Honey, there are plenty of great gluten-free foods," he assured her. "I should have bought some today. I'll grab some of your favorites tomorrow. Is that okay?"

She smiled at him. "Thanks. Will this pass?"

He nodded in assurance. "Get some rest and drink plenty of water. Take it easy for the rest of the day and you should feel better by tomorrow."

He helped her up from her chair and escorted her to her room. True enough, she felt better the next day and by the time Sunday rolled around, she was back to her old self.

Sunday was usually a hectic time in the household but with Kristen's accompanying presence, the family was even more alert than usual.

"We leave in less than an hour. How are you guys doing?" Mark's voice carried through the house from downstairs.

"Almost ready!" Jasmine hollered back.

She popped in a CD and soon the soundtrack to *Cinderella* filled the upstairs hall. Ilene Wood's voice began to sing "A Dream is a Wish Your Heart Makes" and Kristen couldn't help but sing along, the movie scene ingrained in her memory.

"...No matter how your heart is grieving, if you keep on believing, the dream that you wish will come true."

Jasmine joined in. As the pace began to quicken, they began to dance and twirl in the hall, humming the tune loudly. Kylie rushed up the stairs with her dad and immediately joined in. Mark looked on and smiled as his wife and daughters danced to the old song. The girls twirled circles around their mother and Jasmine at one point began to waltz with her.

He glanced to the right and saw his son standing at the threshold of his room, watching his mom and sisters. He smiled the faintest of smiles and looked almost longingly on the scene, as if wishing he could somehow join in the spontaneous bonding. He caught his father watching him and immediately wiped the smile off his face before stepping back into his room. Mark sighed. He had to figure out a way to get Caleb to open up and reconcile with her. The song ended and a much slower track started to play. The ladies stopped dancing and looked around as if clueless on what to do next. Kristen caught Mark's eyes on her as he finished walking up the stairs. He wordlessly took out the *Cinderella* CD and replaced it with *The Princess and the Frog* soundtrack. Immediately, "Almost There" began to play and the girls resumed their dancing.

They would probably be late for church but he didn't mind anymore.

They pulled up to the bustling parking lot and quickly found a spot. The kids hopped out, eager to see their friends but Mark and Kristen held back for a moment.

"Are you sure you're okay?" he asked. She looked around at the surroundings and nodded. Trees lined the property and there were several buildings on what appeared to be the same lot of land. Mark had explained that there was a network of churches working together and they attended one of them: Oasis Church. Their church was in a medium-sized building with a dome in the center. It wasn't ostentatious or imposing but looked rather inviting. It was like everything else to her, foreign but nonthreatening.

He grabbed her hand and rubbed it softly.

"I'm with you, okay?"

She smiled in appreciation and opened her door. Mark met her halfway around the other side of the car and took her hand again. They crossed the lot and entered the foyer together and Kristen immediately realized why he was nervous for her. No sooner had they set foot in the church, when a sea of friendly faces inundated the couple.

"Kristen! Mark! We're so happy to see you!"

"Thank God she's alive!"

"Kristen, we've missed you so much!"

"You look beautiful!"

"How are you adjusting?"

"Do you need meals? We can do a rotation."

"How are the kids adjusting?"

"Do you remember me?"

That last one irritated her the most. She knew they meant well, but every single person who approached her in familiar warmth was a complete stranger to her. Thankfully, Mark handled the majority of the inquisition and kept her hand firmly in his own. When it was time for the service to begin, he wrapped his arm around her waist and escorted her from the crowd and into the sanctuary. She tried to ignore the pleasure that ran through her at the feel of him holding her possessively. She was grateful that he took the lead and felt protected. She knew she could handle them on her own if she needed to but was grateful that she didn't have to.

Mark searched the crowd and found their daughter towards the center of the sanctuary. The younger ones were in Sunday school. He could feel the stares of the members as he led Kristen to their seats. He knew it was out of curiosity and happiness on their part but he also knew they were unwittingly putting his wife on edge. They reached Jasmine and sat to her right. Jasmine immediately jostled to sit in between them and Mark reluctantly gave up his spot next to Kristen. He knew Jasmine was eager to be closer to her mom and he could tell she helped put her mother at ease in most settings.

The lights dimmed as the praise and worship began. Kristen began to feel more at ease as the lights made it more difficult for people to watch her, her husband included. She appreciated his concern for her but she could also feel his eyes drifting to her direction often and she just needed to be left alone. Jasmine was the only person who treated her like a normal individual and the tenderness she felt towards her grew.

God, what are you doing here? she thought. *I'm so out of my element even in your house.*

The first two songs were foreign to Kristen and she was about to sit the third one out when she heard a familiar chord. The band started playing "Be Still, My Soul" and her heart lifted. She immediately began to sing along and her spirit lightened. She closed her eyes and let the notes and the lyrics surround her. Hands raised, she abandoned her thoughts, her worries, and everything in that moment to the Lord, grateful for the reprieve. At the bridge of the song, the band paused and the church sang acapella. She heard a strong, tenor voice to her left, past Jasmine's sweet soprano, and glanced at Mark. His eyes were closed and his hands were raised. She could make out the glistening around his eye lashes as he sang from deep within his core. He sang like he knew his Creator from the inside out. He sang like a man who had been *through it* in the worst possible way. Come to think of it, wasn't he going through it then? With an amnesiac wife and three kids to care for? Transfixed by the image of her husband fervently praising God, she felt a new admiration for him grow. The music ended and she continued to watch as he kept his eyes closed and basked in the afterglow of worship. His expression full of peace, he opened his eyes and, as if sensing her gaze, turned to catch her eyes. She quickly looked away.

The service was a short, direct one. The pastor, a middle-aged Asian man, gave a sermon entitled, "God's Crazy Glue: Putting the Pieces Back Together." The sermon revolved around God redeeming every situation, raising the phoenix from the ashes, and making sense of what seemed senseless to the world. He could never know how fitting it was to Mark and Kristen in that moment. Kristen in particular felt chills go down her spine when he read Romans 8:28 - the same verse that came to her in the hotel room in New York:

"And we know that in all things God works for the good of those who love him..."

If you're trying to tell me something, Kristen thought, *I'm listening. If this situation can become a phoenix in the ashes, please let it be so.*

"I want a cheeseburger too!" Kylie said excitedly.

They were all sitting in a booth at a 1950s style diner, sipping on milkshakes and talking about the service. It was a circular booth with Mark and Caleb seated opposite Kristen, Kylie and Jasmine - Kristen wedged between the two girls. Much of the congregation had tried to jockey towards the family for a chance to see Kristen but Mark had managed to round up the kids quickly after service and take them out to lunch, promising to reconnect with their church community later in the month. Their food arrived in less than fifteen minutes and the kids dug in immediately.

Jasmine glanced at Kristen and asked around her burger, "What did you think of it?"

"The service?"

"The church," she clarified.

Kristen nodded. "I really like it. The music was good, the sermon was encouraging and the people there are really kind." She looked around at them and asked, "How long have we been going there?"

Mark smiled at her choice of words. "We started going shortly after Caleb's birth."

"Hey!" Caleb protested as Kylie nabbed a small handful of his fries.

Kylie giggled mischievously and offered her brother some of her strawberry milkshake. Caleb reluctantly grinned and took a sip. Kristen watched the exchange and smiled. Though the two got on each other's nerves occasionally, it was easy to see that they liked each other and got along. She glanced at Jasmine and saw her roll her eyes at the pair.

"How's Trig going?" she asked. Jasmine raised her eyebrows in surprise.

"Okay, I guess. I still don't think the teacher knows what she's doing but it isn't making my grade suffer."

Kristen nodded. "Good. I hated Trigonometry. It was the only class I ever got a 'C' in during my entire time in high school."

Jasmine frowned. "Aww, that sucks."

Kristen glanced at Mark, who was smiling.

"Let me guess, you aced it across the board." she remarked.

He shrugged and admitted, "For every 'A' I got in Trig, I struggled to make it in English and Lit."

"Would you say you're more of a left-brain person or a right-brain person?" Kristen asked Jasmine.

"What does that mean?" Kylie asked. Mark explained it to her while Jasmine answered Kristen.

"Hmm, I actually think I'm both. I do really well in Math *and* English. I like to problem solve but I also enjoy painting."

"What do you want do when you grow up?"

For the first time, Kristen saw a look of anxiety cross her daughter's face.

"I don't know. Before you left..." The table quieted. "You were trying to help me figure it out. I took some assessments and stuff but we couldn't pinpoint a career."

Mark looked between the two of them. He knew Jasmine would be successful in whatever she chose to do but he had understood Kristen's concern to get her going in some sort of direction. Jasmine looked down at her plate, her appetite suddenly gone.

"Hey."

She felt a gentle hand touch her arm and she looked back up at her mom.

"Don't worry about it. You still have time to figure it out and it might just come down to trying a bunch of different things before you find your sweet spot."

Jasmine looked at her with her mouth wide open; it slowly transformed into a smile and a look of relief washed over her countenance. Mark smiled, happy at the turn in the conversation. Though he had understood Kristen's previous determination, he was grateful that the pressure was off their daughter. He wondered if it had anything to do with her mindset. A twenty-six-year-old saw life's years as eons ahead of them, while a thirty-seven-year-old knew how important it was to plan. Jasmine would need a happy medium.

Kylie was tired of that conversation. "Mommy, I don't want you to go to New York."

Mark frowned at his youngest. "Kylie, we already talked about this."

"I know, but I still don't want her to go," she said in her cute, high-pitched voice.

Kristen smiled, "I'll be back the same night, though. You won't even notice I'm gone."

"And it's live, so we can root her on as she talks," Jasmine pointed out. The reminder made Kristen swallow hard. She had grown used to pre-recorded shows and hadn't done a live broadcast in quite some time.

Mark watched her closely and could see the gamut of anxiety in her eyes. He turned to his kids.

"Let's pray for your mom's panel tomorrow."

Jasmine nodded and Kylie immediately reached out for her mom and dad's hands. Caleb said nothing but silently held Jasmine and his father's hands. Kristen smiled at Mark in appreciation before they bowed their heads and Mark began to pray.

"Lord, we lift up Kristen to you. Please be with her as she travels to New York tomorrow for Carissa Perry's panel. Please keep her focused and attentive and allow her to relax during the whole taping. Let her have fun and impress her co-workers and all those around her. Give her a safe journey before, during, and after the panel trip and bless her meeting with ABC. We know she can do it and we thank you that you empower her to do all things through you. We love her and we love you. In Jesus' name, amen."

The kids echoed with a resounding, "Amen!" that drew the attention of several patrons.

"Thank you, guys." Kristen said, touched.

"You got this, Mom. You're gonna kill it out there!" Jasmine replied.

Kristen smiled at them all before meeting Mark's eyes again.

"Thank you," she mouthed.

"You're welcome," he mouthed in return.

CHAPTER SEVEN
The Sadness

New York, New York

Kristen strode into the studio, the confident click of her heels hiding the nervous beat of her heart. The trip to the city had been pretty straightforward. She had appreciated going without Mark this time. It made her feel grown up and in charge. She had traveled before as a young adult and could vividly remember her previous trips into cities by plane. It was one of those little things that built her confidence the closer she got to the impending panel.

Now she was here.

Her meeting with ABC had gone smoothly. The ratings were high and people were regularly tuning in but the studio wanted to find ways to increase viewership as usual and they too thought this was a great way to do it.

"Kristen!"

A petite woman of ambiguous lineage greeted her with an extended hand. Kristen knew from previous research that this was indeed Carissa Perry, star of the Carissa Perry Show. She was pretty, with caramel skin, light hazel eyes, and medium curly brown hair. They shook hands.

"I'm a huge fan. Thank you so much for agreeing to do this."

Kristen smiled, showing no hint of nerves. "I'm glad to be of service. This should be fun."

Carissa nodded in affirmation.

After meeting the producer and other panelists briefly, Kristen went to her dressing room to do makeup. A production assistant went over the key notes of the panel discussion and briefed her on the layout of the cameras. Kristen then waited in a private greenroom and tried to still her nerves. She felt her body tingle on all ends. She closed her eyes and almost immediately pictured herself in the diner from the day before, hands joined as Mark prayed over this very moment. A feeling of calm washed over her just as the door opened.

"Mrs. Tyverson? We're ready for you."

They got seated during the commercial break. To her right, was a well-known female comedienne, to her left, an actor and beside him, a fellow news show host. Carissa went through the introductions quickly and dove right into the topics.

"Okay, the recession. How are we doing as a nation right now? According to economists, there is a huge scare over the number of citizens whose unemployment benefits will end next month. The question begs: are we out of the recession yet?"

Kristen quickly got the hang of things. Each panelist started out the discussion by answering the question and jumped in as they would any normal conversation. Because she had researched the topics well in advance, Kristen was able to give well-informed, thoughtful answers. And unlike several of her co-panelists, she managed to support her assertions with several credible sources. She could see the familiar expressions: surprise dissolving into admiration as she tackled each topic adeptly; from the economy to politics to diplomacy.

"Okay, our final topic of the segment: celebrity news." Carissa announced. "According to Time Magazine columnist, Stuart Jameson,

Americans in general are becoming dumber with the increasing exposure and obsession with celebrities. Does he have a point?"

The actor to her left immediately balked. "Of course not. I find that people who write articles like this have some sort of complex about attractive, talented people gaining more attention than they do."

The comedienne to her right agreed.

"I don't know," the other journalist countered. "There is reason to examine the intellect of our society, especially when compared to the innovation and drive of countries like China or Japan. The U.S. has fallen in the ranks of so many world arenas and it might be fair to say it is because of our preoccupation with stars and their exploits as opposed to, I don't know, trying to get a man on the moon."

Kristen nodded. "I agree. How many kids today can name all of our state capitals much less identify the geography of the rest of the world? How many Americans are familiar with the work of Leo Tolstoy as opposed to the latest news from the Kartrashians?"

Carissa's jaw dropped. Kristen frowned.

What did I say?

She quickly re-ran her sentence through her mind and immediately realized her mistake.

"Excuse me, I meant the Kardashians. I'm sorry." Though her voice was composed, Kristen felt heat rise to her face and her stomach cramped as she vaguely noticed the red recording light on all of the cameras. It was too late. She couldn't pull that statement back in or have it edited out or re-do what she said. The broadcast was live and she just called one of the most famous families in the world *trash* on national air.

Carissa quickly gave her thoughts on the subject and wrapped up the discussion but Kristen had already checked out. She couldn't *believe* she had slipped up like that. It was one thing to joke about the name with Jasmine or read about it in comments below articles but to actually articulate it on national television?

When they went off air, Kristen stood, eager to leave. She shook hands with the fellow panelists and did her best to accommodate the niceties.

With the exception of the actor, all of them, including Carissa, told her not to worry about the slip up. She smiled tightly and thanked them for having her. Regardless of what they said, she could feel the eyes and hear the whispers of the crew and production team around her. As soon as she reached her phone in the dressing room, she saw the trending headline:

"KRISTEN TYVERSON CALLS KARDASHIAN FAMILY 'TRASH.'"

There was an onslaught of instant articles and news feeds, re-playing and highlighting her "Kartrashian" slip-up over and over again. They must have started writing the articles the second the word came out of her mouth.

This new media - which she was still coming to grips with, was suddenly walloping her across the head. What did this mean for her job? For her reputation as a journalist? Katie Couric and Anderson Cooper may have been comfortable giving their opinions on celebrities, but Kristen still valued the old-school tradition of absolute objectivity. She'd never heard Walter Cronkite or Dan Rather comment on the lives of celebrities when they were alive.

She quickly gathered her things and headed to the lobby to catch her car service to the JFK airport. To her horror, she was met with a tide of paparazzi cameras. She kept her head down but there weren't earplugs strong enough to keep her from hearing the rude questions and comments.

"Kristen, why did you call the Kardashians trash?"

"How long have you hated the Kardashian family?"

"Kristen, is this how ABC views the famous clan?"

"Did your amnesia cause you to mess up on air?"

"Kristen, what do you think about the Khloe and Lamar divorce?"

"Kanye West just blasted you on twitter. Any thoughts?"

She fastened herself into the car and watched the New Yorkers stride across the concrete streets and sidewalks. The press was gone but she knew that, that was just a taste of the repercussions of her slip. The silence in the car was pierced every now and then with the beeping of her phone. She silenced it. She couldn't bear to see more alerts.

I apologized on air - just seconds after I slipped. Why won't they let this go?

She wanted to hide and retreat to her thoughts but that wasn't going to happen anytime soon.

The airport was swarming with press and she barely made it to her plane in time. Even in first class, she could hear the whispers and feel the stares of the fellow passengers when she wanted nothing more than to disappear from sight.

"Kids, it's time for bed."

Kristen turned the key and entered the house, surprised to see most of the lights still on. She walked down the hall to find all three kids on the family computer, reading the articles about the slip-up online.

"'Kanye West reportedly tweeted: 'Hate on me but don't talk about my girl. Screw you, KT.'" Jasmine recited.

"'KT?'" Kylie asked.

"Kristen Tyverson," she explained. She sighed. "I don't know why they won't let it go. It was a simple mistake. Besides, the Kardashians *are* trash. Mom!"

All three heads snapped to her direction. Kylie sprinted over to Kristen and threw herself into her arms. Jasmine stood up to greet her as well but Caleb stayed at the computer, continuing to read the article.

Heavy footsteps quickly entered the foyer and for a moment, all Kristen could see were Mark's eyes. A look of anxiety clouded them, silently asking her: *are you alright?*

It was too much.

She could hardly stand the embarrassment on set. The paparazzi had rattled her nerves; and the never-ending wave of articles and social media made her stomach turn. She didn't know what awaited her with ABC and one of her kids was avidly reading the article once again detailing her national screw up. She glanced at Caleb, still stationed at the computer. Mark followed her gaze and frowned.

"This is what you guys were looking at?"

Jasmine gave a guilty nod. She looked at Kristen.

"Sorry, Mom. For what it's worth, I think you did an amazing job. One little mistake shouldn't overshadow that."

But it did. Instead of talking about how put together and seemingly-recovered Kristen was, they were now calling into question her mental acuity and reputation as a journalist. Her name was forever entangled with a family that was famous for nothing but their sexual and reality TV exploits.

Mark could read her thoughts like a musician reading a score.

"Kids, it's time for bed. *Now.*"

Kylie squeezed Kristen's waist one more time, hugged her father and headed upstairs. Jasmine did the same and Caleb headed straight to the stairs with a barely-spoken "Night."

Mark closed the space between them, hesitantly. Noticing that she didn't stiffen, he slowly wrapped her in his arms.

"You were terrific," he whispered. "Don't let that moment eclipse the entire thing."

She lifted her arms and clung onto his shirt, burying her face in his neck. She breathed in his cologne and allowed the heady scent to comfort her. She pulled back after a few moments, just in time for Kylie to yell in a sing-song voice:

"Daddy! I'm ready for you to tuck me in!"

Kristen smiled weakly and walked upstairs. Mark watched her until she disappeared into her room and then made his way to Kylie's.

In her room, Kristen walked to her small, walk-in closet and flipped on the light. She kicked off her heels, shrugged off her coat and set down her purse. She shook off her suit jacket and out fell her cell phone. Bending to pick it up, Kristen paused.

She caved…and looked at the notifications.

More than sixty missed calls; most from strange numbers; others from contacts she didn't remember making; and quite a few from Lance and other producers at ABC. She clicked on her twitter app and saw a bevy of tweets all with the hashtag "Kartrashians." A feeling of deep sadness and loneliness enveloped her. No one was there in that moment, in her shoes. The one person she could always talk to, to clarify issues and comfort her in a maternal embrace - gone. For the first time in several weeks, the death of Kristen's mother hurt her even deeper than it had the first time she'd learned of it.

The tears prickled painfully at her eyes and nose and a low sob pushed forth like a child coming into the world. The cries came from deep within her throat. She dropped the phone and folded her hands over her eyes as the sobs wracked her body with a force she could not control. Suddenly, strong arms enveloped her shaking frame and pulled her into a solid, warm chest. Mark held her firmly, wordlessly stroking her arms as she cried into his chest, her tears wetting his shirt. He fastened his lips to the top of her head and felt the vibration of her sobs. He felt her arms wrap around his torso as she clung to his shirt and rode out the waves of sorrow.

◯

"I don't know what to do, Reed." Mark admitted over the phone. "She keeps to herself as much as possible and whenever she's not at work or at physical therapy, she's in the gym."

"Body image issues."

"I know but no matter how many times I tell her she's beautiful, she won't let this thing go."

Reed was quiet for a moment.

"While that is disconcerting, I'm more concerned about the depressive mood. Why is she so depressed? Isn't work going well?"

"Yeah, her ratings are higher than ever."

Three weeks had passed since the slip-up on air and both Kristen and Mark had managed to maintain the routine they had established weeks ago. The busy season for Mark's firm had passed and all of his clients were more than happy with their tax refunds. Kristen had survived the storm as well. Despite the instantaneous fallout from her on air mistake, ratings incidentally rose. Her comment struck a chord with the nation and most viewers were delighted to hear their sentiments echoed on national television. The comment was a catalyst for a larger discussion on just *how many* people were sick of hearing and seeing the Kardashians. A petition even took place to get them off the air. There was a stated goal of one million people; they already exceeded five.

To the execs at ABC, it was as if nothing had happened. Much of the media had already moved on to two new stories. But for Kristen, it wasn't over. Though the embarrassment and fear had passed, the entire experience sunk her into a deep depression that neither she nor her family was prepared for. No matter what Kylie or Jasmine did, no matter how often Mark tried to talk to her, Kristen couldn't find it in herself to cheer up and smile.

Mark thought back to that night when he comforted her in the closet.

"After she cried it out, she got really quiet. It was like she was taking in every negative thing anyone said about her segment and she wasn't fighting back. And then, when the whole thing blew over and people had moved on, she still hadn't."

"Does she ever talk to you about what is specifically bothering her?"

"No." He sighed in frustration. "She just keeps to herself and goes through the day like a robot."

"Hmm. Are there any special dates coming up? Any anniversaries or birthdays that you know of?"

Mark frowned at the question. What did that have to do with anythin-?

"Oh God," he said quietly, closing his eyes.

"What?"

He opened them again, horrified at what he'd forgotten.

"Her mom. Her mom's birthday was two weeks ago and the anniversary of her death was a week after that. How could I have forgotten? What on earth was I thinking?"

"Mark, you've been busy. You're not superman and she knows that. Okay, this is good. We have a lead. She misses her mom."

"This whole thing probably amplified the fact that she's gone."

Mark couldn't even begin to imagine how alone Kristen felt. Even when he thought he had lost her, he still had his folks in Texas. He still had his kids. He had remembered everyone in his circle when they tried to rally around him.

Mark ended the call with Reed, took a deep breath and closed his eyes.

Lord, give me wisdom. She's been walking around like an open wound for weeks. How can I help her heal?

Kristen sat in the formal living room and stared off into the neighborhood outside. The sun was quickly going down and the kids outside were heading in for dinner. It still felt surreal to her that she had her *own* kids to think about. They were in the family room, watching TV while Mark made their dinner. Kristen wrapped her arms around herself and tried to figure everything out all at once. It felt like just yesterday, everything was in her control. That she had a choice.

But she had woken up.

Woken up to a life that she didn't understand and couldn't remember choosing.

Do I have a choice now?

She didn't think she did. How do you leave your doting husband and children just because you can't remember signing up for them? And she wasn't sure she even wanted to renege on her commitments. She thought of Mark and how patient, kind and gentle he had been. She thought of Kylie and Jasmine; how they loved her openly without any reservations. Caleb was difficult to read but she knew that on some level, even he was deeply affected by her return. She was important to these people. She had a family; just not the family she had expected and remembered.

The dust had settled on her panel screw up. While she wished it had never happened, there was nothing she could do to change it. She knew it was irrational, but the whole experience made her yearn for her mother all the more. And as her birthday and death anniversary passed with nary a soul in the house noticing except her, she wished more than anything that her mother was still alive; that she could talk to her and get her advice on how to move forward - how to interact not only with her children but also her husband.

As patient as Mark was being, Kristen knew he desired her as his wife. She didn't miss the intimate glances and flashes of lust that passed his expression every now and then. Being around him, she felt more aware of her body than she ever had before. And while part of her enjoyed the attention of such an attractive man, another part of her felt even more self-conscious about the differences in her body. She had literally woken up to a new, heavier body and her workouts weren't changing things as quickly as she wanted them to.

And then there was work.

A massive career with almost all of her goals accomplished and she couldn't remember a bit of the success. In college, she used to wish she could just fast forward past her struggles and land in to her thirties, where the money was rolling in and the finances were stable. While she enjoyed not worrying over every purchase and lived quite comfortably, Kristen wished she could remember the sensation of rising to the top of her field. What did it feel like to get that key promotion? What did it look like when she first walked into the studio in *New York City*? How did she react when she got her first significant pay raise?

How did I feel on my wedding day?

The thought came out of nowhere. Before she could analyze it further, two little pink-slippered feet approached her with precocious steps. Kylie slowly and carefully walked towards Kristen, her eyes fixed on the ceramic mug filled with hot chocolate. She held it out to her mother with a proud glint in her blue eyes.

"Daddy said I could give it to you as long as I was *super* careful."

Kristen took the mug and looked past Kylie to find Mark watching them from the kitchen, a dish towel thrown over his shoulder as he continued to make dinner.

"He said he hopes this makes you feel better."

"Thank you, sweetie." Kristen whispered as she watched her husband.

When he saw that the drink had been safely delivered, he gave his wife a brief smile and returned to the meal. *Please let that lift her spirits - even just a little,* he thought. Hot cocoa was her favorite, any time of the year.

Kristen continued to watch Mark in wonder. Even in her sadness and self-absorption, he was taking notice of her and trying to meet her needs. He didn't ask questions. He called Kylie back to him after she had delivered the drink, respecting Kristen's need for some time alone. And yet he was still comforting her just by the mere gesture. Showing her he cared.

She sipped the warm drink and listened as he finished preparing dinner and rounded up the kids to eat. She listened to him as he asked each child about their day and how they were doing. All of them, Caleb included, spoke freely with their dad about school, friends, and any concerns they had. She could tell they felt completely comfortable around him. He was an incredibly attentive and understanding father.

Am I capable of being that kind of a mother?

When the dinner was finished and the dishes cleaned, the kids went back to doing homework or watching TV. Mark made his way to the formal living room and hesitated at the threshold. Kristen smiled at him.

"You can come in," she said quietly. He did.

He pointed at her empty mug. "Can I take that for you?"

Kristen shook her head and patted the seat beside her. He gave a brief look of surprise before taking a seat. Kristen gestured to the mug.

"Thank you for this. It was really sweet of you."

"Not a problem. I'm sorry we forgot to acknowledge Thelma's birthday."

She inhaled sharply and Mark reached out to hold her hand. She accepted it and he rubbed the back of it in gentle circles. She shook her head in frustration.

"I don't know why I can't snap out of it, you know?"

Mark shook his head. "No, I don't know."

Kristen looked at him, frowning.

"You've been through so much. How can anyone expect you to just 'snap out of it'? I mean, what are you supposed to snap out of? Not remembering? Feeling confused? Hurting? I don't think you snap out of those things. I think you go through it with those who love you."

Her chin trembled and she looked down at their hands, dark and fair fingers intertwined.

He waited for her to say something and when she didn't, he used his other hand to pull her into his side. She laid her head against his chest and listened to his heart beat in a steady, soothing rhythm. It wasn't the first time she had found comfort in his arms.

"I made a good choice," she finally said. "You're a really good man."

"I have an even better woman."

She smiled. "Tell me more about yourself. What's your favorite movie?"

"Of all the topics to pick, you choose movies?"

"I love movies," she said.

"I know you do," he countered.

She laughed. It was the first time in a long time he'd heard that sound come from her and he reveled in it.

"I can't choose a favorite. I have too many."

"Name some of them."

"Okay. I like *Ordinary People, The Godfather…*"

Kristen nodded her head in agreement as he continued.

"*Legends of the Fall, Aliens, The Firm, It Happened One Night, Inception-*"

"*Inception?*" she briefly lifted her head to look at him. His brown eyes were relaxed, happy. She put her head back down as he answered, enjoying the vibration in his chest as he spoke in his baritone voice.

"Oh yeah, it came out in 2010. You loved it when we first went to see it. It's definitely a mind-bender."

"Do you know my favorite movie?" she asked.

"Yes. And it *still* hasn't changed in all these years. *Titanic-*"

"*Yes!* I *adore* that movie!"

"You like anything by James Cameron," he pointed out.

"I do. *Aliens* was amazing and *The Terminator* still gives me chills. Has he released any new movies since *Titanic?*"

Mark nodded. "In 2009, he came out with *Avatar*. It beat the box office draw for *Titanic* and is now the highest grossing film of all time. You loved it when it came out."

"What's it about?"

Mark told her the basic plot without revealing any spoilers - even though she begged him to.

"What's the fun of watching a movie if you know what's going to happen?" he asked.

"Spoilers don't ruin movies for me. I want to know what happens *now*!"

"Then watch the movie. You spoil too many good stories by looking them up on Wikipedia beforehand."

She smiled and enjoyed the warmth of his chest.

"So I have to watch *Avatar*, you said I would like *Inception*. Jasmine thinks I should see the *Bourne* trilogy."

"Ah, you're going to *love* those movies. The *Bourne* films are so well written and made."

"I've missed out on so much."

He rubbed her shoulder.

"Baby steps. What's most important is that you're here."

She nodded, finally agreeing with that assessment. No matter how down she felt, she knew it was a miracle she was alive. Mark and their family were no longer the only ones grateful.

"It's interesting seeing how things have changed. Even on the political stage. I never imagined politicians could get even more contentious. We've progressed and regressed all at the same time."

"How so?" he asked.

"Well, we have a black President. I never thought I'd see that in my lifetime. But we also have a Congress that is unable to agree over the smallest decisions. I mean, how can you allow a political debate to degenerate so poorly to the point where you have to shut down an entire government? It's disgusting."

"It is. Today's politicians have become some of the nastiest, unscrupulous individuals in the world and the sad thing is they are making decisions that affect us all."

"The lobbying is out of control. Can you imagine how much corruption would be cut if it were illegal to lobby politicians at all levels?"

"You're preaching to the choir," Mark replied, kissing her forehead. Her heart fluttered at the affectionate gesture.

"Mark, what are you?" she finally asked. He was surprised that she had held off for so long.

"I'm an independent," he answered. "Not conservative but not quite as liberal as you, I'm afraid."

"Abortion?"

"Pro-life."

"Rape and incest?"

"Those are exceptions."

"Obamacare?"

"If it were structured like Canadian or British health care, I would be on board. The early form of the public option was really appealing to me. But I think what they have now is a bit of a mess and more people are losing than winning at this point."

"I agree. How can you force an entire population to buy health insurance and then not properly regulate the companies so that they don't screw the population being required to purchase from them? They guaranteed the clientele for the insurers but barely did anything to maximize the power of the patients."

"Exactly," Mark agreed. "What do you think about gay marriage?"

"Wow, we're really getting into it."

"You started it."

She chuckled. "I know. You first, what do you think?"

"I think it's an inevitability in this country. There are too many people pushing for it to happen and it probably will."

"But you're against it?"

"The Bible is clear on it."

"But not everybody agrees with Christianity or lives their lives by the Bible."

Mark nodded. "Exactly – which is why I think it's pointless for people to protest the legalization of gay marriage on the basis of a belief that not all people subscribe to. I'm not on the picket line, supporting Prop Eight and I'm not on the picket line supporting gay marriage. I think of 1 Corinthians 5:9-13. God will be the final judge."

"Amen."

"You agree?"

"I do. I think it's sad that people can't agree to disagree on this particular topic though. As soon as you say anything that doesn't endorse homosexuality, you're branded as a 'homophobe.' People are all for 'tolerance' as long as it doesn't require them to tolerate an opinion they don't agree with."

"You're talking about the Duck Dynasty thing?"

"Don't even get me started on that."

They laughed, enjoying the moment of companionship and camaraderie. So caught up in their conversation were they, that they didn't even notice their kids peeking in on them. Jasmine led the pack and was pleased to find them cozy on the couch, in each other's arms, laughing and talking much like they used to before her mother's accident. She quickly shooed her siblings away, afraid that they would all ruin the moment if discovered by their parents.

Their conversation moved onto lighter topics like sports and television and eventually music. Mark caught Kristen up on some of the latest musicians and even the technology used to play music. As she flipped through his ipod, she was surprised to find a mix of classic rock with new R&B including artists like Miguel and J. Cole. Even his Christian music had a combination of Chris Tomlin and Jesus Culture alongside gospel artists like Fred Hammond and Byron Cage.

By the time she went to bed that night, Kristen felt a deep joy and hope well inside her. She knew her husband on an entirely deeper level. For the first time in a long time, she could point to a moment since waking up and count it as entirely good.

CHAPTER EIGHT
Family Day

The next day started with a bang. Mark was so invigorated from their conversation the previous night that he decided to keep the momentum going. He was determined to continue guiding Kristen out of her depression and self-exile. He surprised the entire family by taking them all to the Clearcrest Recreational Center downtown. Though Kristen couldn't remember, they had been there as a family numerous times, taking turns wall climbing, jumping on trampolines, and doing various activities as a family just for the fun of it.

The kids were game the minute they heard. And though reluctant at first, Kristen joined in, unwilling to ruin their fun - which soon became her own.

"Mommy, look at me!" Kylie called as she did another back flip on the giant trampoline. The little girl sprawled herself into the air fearlessly, her tawny curls flying in all directions.

Kristen immediately applauded her.

"Great job, Ky!" It was nickname that Kristen had gotten into the habit of calling her youngest child. She didn't know if it was something she used to call her and she didn't care. Her daughter didn't seem to mind it.

Jasmine and Mark were enjoying themselves on the inflated obstacle course. They had raced several times, each time coming up neck and neck; pretty impressive for a man in his late thirties. Even Caleb seemed to be having a blast, climbing the ropes as the instructor guided him. He quickly got bored with it, though, and wanted to do the wall climbing activity.

"Sorry, bud. You need to have a partner if you want to do the racing climb."

Caleb looked around the center and saw the rest of his family already occupied. He looked at Kristen and met her eyes.

She asked, "Would you like me to race you?"

He nodded hesitantly and they got geared up to do it. Both remained quiet as the instructors told them how to climb. One of them set a stop watch and yelled out.

"On your mark, get set…go!"

Kristen scaled the wall with relative ease and felt a rush of adrenaline as she saw her son race up the wall, as if he had a rocket strapped to his back. Though she reached the top in pretty good time, Caleb was halfway down the wall by the time she was beginning to descend. When she reached the bottom, the rest of her family had already congregated around Caleb, congratulating him. They cheered her on as she joined them and she immediately felt Mark's arms circle her waist.

"Great job, honey."

"Thanks." She smiled up at him, enjoying the strength in his arms.

She looked down at their son and extended her palm. "You kicked my butt - great job!"

Caleb gave her a small smile and quickly returned her high five.

After the recreation center, the family headed to the mall and enjoyed some food. They decided to make a quick stop at the Family Christian store. The manager, a tall light-skinned man in his forties, warmly greeted Mark by name. He smiled at Kristen and genuinely said, "Welcome back. We missed you."

Kristen smiled, touched. "Thank you."

Kylie and Caleb entertained themselves in the children's section while Jasmine became engrossed with the teen read section. Mark sidled up to Kristen as she stared at the massive wall of Christian novels.

"Are you a Christian fiction fan?" he asked.

She smiled. She loved that he asked her questions that he probably already knew the answer to. He wasn't taking her ideas for granted. He never assumed how she felt about anything.

"Not really." she answered. "I mean, I like Francine Rivers and Jasmine let me borrow a book by Claudia Mair Burney."

"*Zora and Nicky*?"

She turned to him.

"Yeah. I loved that book. It was so well written. Unfortunately, I can't say that for most of the books in that genre."

Mark laughed and nodded.

"I usually just come here for the commentaries and nonfiction."

Together, they selected some devotionals and commentaries they both thought would be interesting to read. Kristen saw several titles in the "Marriage and Family" section and Mark pointed out the ones they already owned. After an hour, they all gathered at the register and made their purchase. Jasmine had convinced her father to get her three novels, a devotional, and a new study Bible, specifically geared for teens her age.

"Would you like your name on it?" the cashier asked in a pleasant tone.

Both parents looked at Jasmine whose face lit up at the suggestion. But she stopped herself, glanced at the register total, wiped off her smile and said, "No, thank you."

"How much is it?" Mark asked.

"Only six dollars."

Jasmine shook her head vehemently.

"No. You've already spent over fifty bucks, just on my stuff. No, thank you."

She turned away and joined her siblings who were looking at a stand with "World Vision" written across the banner.

Kristen reached into her wallet and handed the cashier six dollars and change.

"Put her name on it. A gift from me."

Mark smiled at her, pleased that she made the gesture he was planning on doing anyway.

As the cashier passed the Bible on to the imprinter, Kristen asked him, "Why is she so concerned about the cost?"

Mark glanced at their eldest and surmised, "Before we adopted her, Jasmine was in a foster home that had far too many kids for the foster parents to handle. She said that they always talked about money and how much of a burden the kids were to their expenses."

"Oh, God."

"I know. We've been praying about it for a while and even took her to therapy over it. While she's not as bad as she once was, she sometimes slips into these financial guilt trips."

Kristen looked at Jasmine as she joked with her younger siblings and felt her heart fill with even more affection towards the teenager.

"I'm so glad she's ours."

Mark hid his surprise at her sudden acknowledgment of motherhood. For months, she had kept a semi-distance with the kids. She intellectually acknowledged that they were hers but he hadn't seen her take ownership of her role in their family. It was a fantastic first step.

"I am too," he replied. "I love her." *I love you* he wanted to add but held his tongue.

"Daddy, can we get a kid?" Kylie asked, tugging at her father's pants from behind. They turned in her direction and saw her holding a pamphlet with a picture of a little African boy on the front.

Mark frowned.

"What is this?"

The cashier, seeing the exchange, spoke up. "Family Christian is a nonprofit organization. All the proceeds from your purchase will be going towards the widows and orphans in the states and we're also partnered with World Vision, an organization that provides sponsorship to kids around the world."

She went on to explain how sponsoring a child would provide them with food, health care, an education, and the chance to hear the gospel.

"Can people write to the kids?" Kristen asked.

"Absolutely," the cashier responded. "Some even go out to meet their child in person on arranged trips."

"Wow," Mark murmured. He opened the pamphlet and read more about the history of the organization. It had been in existence for over sixty-three years and continued strong long after the founder's death. He particularly liked that the organization worked with the entire village and didn't leave a child behind in the opportunity to get an education and the other resources that they needed. The cost was thirty-five a month and covered everything.

As Mark read the organization literature, the cashier shared her experience of sponsoring a child and Kristen and the other kids listened in rapt attention. The manager joined the discussion and admitted that he too sponsored a child and so did his teenage daughter.

"Some of these kids go on to name their own children after their sponsors because they made such a difference in their lives. My little boy, Ibrahim, lost his father at a young age and his mother doesn't earn enough to stay afloat. He now has a real chance to go to college and rise out of poverty."

Always one to get to the point, Kylie turned to Kristen and finally asked the magic question. "So can we do it?"

"It's up to your dad."

Kristen wanted to but she watched as her husband looked over at the table of more than thirty kids waiting for sponsorship. She didn't want to sign them up for something he wasn't game for.

"Daddy, can we do it?" Kylie asked again.

The cashiers, manager, and kids looked at him in rapt attention. The moment of suspense could be cut with a knife. He turned to Kylie and held up the pamphlet.

"Do you want this little boy?"

She nodded vehemently, her curls bouncing around her face.

"Okay, he's yours."

The staff broke out in applause.

"Praise God! Thank you for rescuing the life of a child."

"Oh, we're not done yet," Mark replied. He turned to Jasmine and Caleb. "You two pick out a child as well."

Kristen's jaw dropped, as did the staff's.

"You want to sponsor *three* kids?" the cashier asked in astonishment.

"Yep. One for each of our kids. We can do this as a family."

Jasmine and Caleb quickly returned with their own pamphlets; they'd each had a child in mind. Kylie picked a little boy from Ethiopia, two months younger than her. Jasmine picked a girl from India, two years younger than her, and Caleb picked a boy from Albania, five years older than him. The manager was so overcome with joy he walked around the register, reached out to Mark and pulled him into a big hug.

"Thank you, Brother. It takes a big heart to sponsor *one* much less three."

Kristen couldn't agree more. A feeling of awe and pride unlike anything she had felt before welled in her heart as she watched her husband fill out the forms for each of the sponsor children. His generosity amazed her. Kylie and Caleb chatted incessantly about their kids and how they couldn't wait to write to them.

The cashier handled the rest of the transaction. "Your new total is twelve dollars and forty-six cents."

Mark's head popped up. "What?"

The cashier nodded. "We reward customers with a twenty dollar discount for every child they sponsor. You sponsored three so we're bringing your total down from seventy-two dollars and forty-six cents to twelve dollars and forty-six cents as a thank you."

The cashier finished ringing up Mark's purchase, processed the sponsor kid forms and handed Jasmine her newly imprinted Bible. Jasmine's mouth dropped at the sight of her name beautifully inscribed on the front of the leather. She looked at her dad who in turn pointed to her mom.

"I wanted you to have it," Kristen said softly.

Jasmine squealed in delight and pulled her mom into her arms.

"Thank you!"

They all walked out of the store with huge grins on their faces, the kids clinging to their sponsor child pamphlets. Kristen could hear one of the staff members comment, "What a beautiful family. I love it when the *real* Christians come in."

⚜

That night, after dinner, the gang congregated around the coffee table in the family room. TV off, they laid out all of the sponsor children pamphlets and wrote their first letters to the kids.

"You guys realize this is a commitment, right? These are *your* pen pals so don't slack on writing letters to them and answering their questions."

The kids nodded, with very serious expressions.

"What should we write in a first letter?" Jasmine asked.

Kristen answered. "Introduce yourself to them and tell them a little about what you like to do and what some of your favorite things are. Tell them how excited you are to sponsor and write to them."

Mark nodded and added, "Ask them some more about themselves and what they need prayer for."

"How do we know if they're believers?" Jasmine asked.

"We don't." Mark glanced at one of the pamphlets. "So ask them if they are and see what they say. If they're not, then you can share the gospel with them."

"They won't get offended?" Caleb quietly asked. It was a very thoughtful question for a nine-year-old boy.

"They're not Americans," Kristen pointed out. "I think they might be more receptive to hearing about Christ. And whether they are or not, you should make sure you at least tried to share the gospel. If they accept it – great. If not, don't push it but pray for them."

The kids nodded, liking that answer. They got down to the task of writing their letters and were quiet for the most part, except to ask how to spell a couple words.

Kristen took the time to marvel at how different the children were, just in their writing styles. Jasmine looked like she was writing the great

American novel while Caleb wrote six short lines and was busy drawing an airplane at the bottom of his letter. Kylie was painstakingly writing out her words, a look of utter concentration furrowing her brows in her cute, chubby face. She signed her name in careful print and drew a heart next it. Placing her pen down, she looked up at her father, who smiled and met her eyes.

"Daddy? Why does God send people to hell if he loves them?"

Kristen's mouth dropped. Jasmine and Caleb both looked up from their letters and Mark raised an eyebrow in surprise. No one could have expected such a question at that time, particularly from a five-year-old little girl. The family watched Mark as he rubbed the back of his neck, carefully measuring his answer.

"That's a good question, sweetie. God loves all people because he created them but as a holy God, he cannot tolerate sin and evil. If he allowed everyone to get into Heaven, including those with sin, he wouldn't be able to co-exist with the sin because he is perfect and good. That's where Jesus comes in. When Jesus died on the cross, he gave sinners the chance to be free of their sin so that they can join God in Heaven and he can have a relationship with them."

Kylie frowned at the table, processing her father's words like a professor processing a complicated thesis.

"You know, your mom got her minor in Biblical Studies." Kristen looked at Mark in surprise. He smiled slyly. "Maybe she can explain this better than I can."

Kristen pursed her lips and rolled her eyes at his grinning face. She looked at Kylie, who had now fixed her gaze on her. Jasmine and Caleb were listening too.

"The best way I can describe it is like this…pretend this house is Heaven. Everyone wants to get in, right?" The kids nodded. "Well, in order for anyone to get in, they have to be spotless because the house is spotless and if they come in with a bunch of dirt and filth, what will happen to the house?"

"It will get dirty." Kylie said.

Kristen nodded. "Right, and if it gets dirty, what does that mean for the house?"

Jasmine said, "It's ruined. It's no longer a spotless paradise."

"Exactly. As far as God is concerned, we're all filthy - no matter what we've done. Whether it's something as small as a 'white lie' or something as huge as killing someone else. You can't come into his house, Heaven, if you're filthy with sin. So what is the solution?"

"Take a bath." Caleb spoke up for the first time. Kristen smiled at him.

"Absolutely. Everyone has to take a bath before they get in. But they can't clean themselves. You know why?"

"Why?" Kylie asked.

"Because there isn't a soap bar strong enough to get rid of all that filth. They have to have a special cleanser."

"What is it?" Kylie asked.

"Christ's blood," Jasmine answered.

"Ding! Ding! Ding!" Kristen exclaimed. "When Jesus died, he took off all the filth and put it on himself. In return, when we believe in him, we are all clean and can enter God's house, spotless."

Kylie smiled as Kristen continued.

"To answer your question, while God loves all people, some people choose not to believe in Jesus or accept the cleanser he offers. So they can't come into his house and the only other place available is…?"

"Hell." Kylie concluded. Kristen nodded.

"That's sad," Caleb said, quietly.

"It is," Mark agreed. "But he loves and respects people too much to force them to do what they should do, even if it's good for them. So pray for the ones who won't listen. That's all you can do."

He turned to Kristen and smiled.

"That was an excellent example. Good job, honey."

Kristen smiled at the endearment. It didn't escape her that this was the second time he'd called her by it that day. "Thanks. Not bad for someone who got put on the spot, huh?"

"I like putting you on the spot. It keeps you on your toes." Mark grinned at her. She held his gaze and grinned back; finding him incredibly attractive in that moment.

"Wow, Dad, you got game." Jasmine remarked. "Look at you two flirting away."

She made eyes at her siblings and they giggled beside her. Kristen laughed openly and Mark chuckled as he felt the telltale heat rush to his face. He wasn't surprised when the next words pointed it out.

"Aww, Dad's blushing now!" Kylie teased. Caleb and Jasmine pointed at their dad's reddened face and joined in the teasing. He threw his hands up to his cheeks; Kristen didn't know if it was to reduce the heat or hide the color.

"Okay, you can stop now!" he said, smiling in good humor.

They didn't, of course, and kept going until the blush disappeared on its own.

When it came time for bed, the girls hugged and kissed both parents good night. Caleb gave his most pleasant good night to Kristen yet and the evening was ending on a general upswing. As Mark tucked Kylie and Caleb in, Kristen stood at the kitchen island and thought to herself, *What a perfect day. Nothing went amiss.*

"Yay, they're out of the way." Mark joked from behind. She smiled at the sound of his voice and turned to face him. He had changed into a dark blue sweater that complimented the muscles in his broad shoulders and strong back. His solid upper body tapered into a solid, trim torso down to long, muscular legs. Realizing she was staring, she quickly met his eyes and saw a hint of a smile cross his face.

"Did you have fun today?" he asked.

She smiled. "I did. I'm so glad you decided to do this."

He nodded. "I am too. All I wanted was to see you smile."

It was the sweetest thing anyone had ever said to her. And yet for some reason, it made her feel uncomfortable. She tried to deflect it and laughed it off.

"Is that what you tell all your guests?" she teased.

He immediately frowned. "You're not a guest."

She looked down at her hands, away from his probing gaze. Why did she say that? In that moment, she knew that she had just taken a perfect day and flushed it down the toilet.

I can't get anything right.

"Is that how you feel? After all this time? Like a guest in your own home?"

She had hurt him and she could see it written in his eyes.

She began to move away from him. "Forget I said anything. I'm sorry, I didn't mean to-"

"Don't apologize. Kristen, I want you to be honest with me. I want to know what's going on in your heart. Are you uncomfortable here? And if so, what can I do to assure you, you belong?"

"Oh, come on, Mark. You and I both know that I don't belong." Kristen snapped finally. She saw him wait for her to elaborate so she did. "I don't *know* you. Not really. We talked politics and movies but I still find it hard to believe that we're married. That we shared our most intimate thoughts with each other. That we've *been* intimate with each other."

Her words were tearing at him but he kept silent and allowed her to continue. He needed to know what the problem was, whether it hurt him or not.

"Your kids-"

"Our kids," he corrected. She had just taken ownership of her role as a mother. He wasn't going to let her give it back.

"These kids-"

"Our kids," he insisted.

She threw her hands up and turned to walk away but he grabbed her shoulders and turned her around.

"Don't do this. Keep going and tell me exactly how you feel."

"What's the point? You keep interrupting me!" The statement threw him for a moment. It was the same thing she often said during their first year of marriage. *You keep interrupting me.* He closed his eyes for a moment and then met hers. They were full of frustration anxiety, distrust and…guilt? She felt just as bad as he did. It was his job to lead them back to a place of trust. He took a deep breath and humbled himself.

"I'm sorry." he said quietly. "I want to hear what you have to say. Always. But those kids aren't just mine and they aren't just kids; they're *ours* - yours and mine - whether you remember it or not."

She looked contrite. "You're right. I'm sorry. It's just…it's been weeks and I'm not remembering anything. I don't remember you or them or our life together. I don't *feel* like a mother. I feel like a twenty-six year old who got placed in some time machine and stepped out at the wrong time."

"So everything that happened at the rec center, at the store, this evening at home? You didn't feel like a mom in those moments?"

She thought hard about it and tried to recall exactly how she felt.

"I - I don't know! They call me 'Mom.' I know I'm their mom but when I talk to them, I feel like I'm talking to really nice kids who I love. I…I…"

She rubbed her forehead in frustration, a gesture he'd seen her do more than a thousand times and he couldn't help but smile.

"What?" she asked. He shook his head and looked at her hands. When he met her eyes again, he fixed her with a tender gaze.

"You're still you, Kristen." he finally said. "You don't remember much and yes, you've lost a lot of the wisdom you'd gained over these eleven years. But at the core, you are *still* you. You're still the woman I fell in love with all those years ago. And I love you now."

She looked away from the heat of his gaze but he gently held her chin and turned her gaze back to his. They held each other's eyes and began to draw together like magnets. He leaned down and quickly claimed her lips. She gasped in surprise but didn't pull away. Her lips were soft and inviting and he deepened the kiss. Within moments, she reached up and pulled him closer to her as he held her at her waist. A feeling of exhilaration suffused her senses and made her feel lightheaded. She felt his tightly muscled arms hold her secure. Heart pounding, he got lost in the heady scent of her hair conditioner. He hadn't meant to kiss her but there was no way he was going to stop now. The kiss started slow and remained that way as both explored one another and re-learned what the other liked. Kristen allowed her hands to explore his body, caressing his arms, shoulders, and the planes of his tightly corded back. By the time they pulled away, both were gasping for air.

Mark met her eyes again and simply said, "You are not a guest."

∼∽⃝

"How are things going, Mark?"

"Where do I begin? She still doesn't remember us, so not too well."

Dr. Longinow asked, "How are things with the kids?"

He nodded quickly. "Good. Really good. She gets along with the girls seamlessly. Caleb was having a hard time of it at first but I can tell it's only a matter of time before he warms up to her again."

"That must give her some hope."

He shook his head. "It should. You think it would…but she's still having a hard time seeing herself as a mom. The kids will ask her permission for something or her opinion and nine times out of ten, she'll look at me for an answer. I keep telling her they're *our* kids but at the same time, how can I blame her? She doesn't even remember having them."

He looked at the beige lamp seated next to Dr. Longinow.

"How is her mood in general? Is she still depressed?"

"No, not since we talked that evening. And the family date last week really cheered her up. The kids too."

"There are other issues?" she asked.

He nodded, visibly bothered. "She's not comfortable in her skin. She's been leaving for the gym every morning at four and doesn't come back until close to seven. She keeps pinching her stomach and looking at herself in the mirror."

Dr. Longinow saddened. "She's regressed. She doesn't remember any of the work we did on that issue. Have you told her that you know?"

"About what happened to her? No. I don't think she would react very well at this point."

She nodded in agreement. She then leaned in and asked intently, "How are the two of you doing? Together?"

He shrugged. "We get along fine. Like roommates. She's polite to me and very considerate of the kids."

"There's been no intimacy, then?"

Mark paused for a moment. When he looked back at the therapist, he saw nothing but compassion and concern in her eyes. So he decided to be honest.

He shook his head. "I want her. Badly." He looked down in embarrassment. "I'm restraining myself the best I can but I can tell she feels uncomfortable around me. I'm still the strange guy that kissed her on the lawn."

He decided not to tell her about the recent kiss. For all he knew, that was a one-off event. Ever since the kiss, Kristen had acted even more skittish around him and he didn't know where he stood with her. As much as he had enjoyed it, he almost regretted it; the entire family date was eclipsed by that one moment and he wondered if it would have been better not to have kissed her at all.

"Mark, it's perfectly normal to feel sexual frustration in this situation. You haven't been with her-"

"With anyone-"

"—with anyone in what? Four months? I wouldn't be surprised if these urges started before you even realized she was alive."

He shook his head. "They didn't. Not when she was gone. But the minute I saw her on that lawn and realized she was alive, every nerve ending came alive again. I'm not giving up on her. God has given me a second chance to better appreciate and understand her. I love her."

"Don't be afraid to show it."

He looked at Dr. Longinow questioningly.

"Don't be afraid to show it," she repeated. "Mark, I admire your determination to be patient and supportive and you should keep doing that but don't be afraid to act like her husband. Affirm her beauty to her; be honest about your desire for her. Don't push her but let her know you still *want* to be her husband and that she *does* belong with you and the kids."

He nodded, appreciative of the prompting.

When he got home that night, for the first time in months, Mark pulled Kristen into his arms without a moment's hesitation, and held her there. Caught by surprise, she stiffened but after a moment or so, relaxed in his embrace, no longer a "guest" in the home.

CHAPTER NINE
More Relaxed

"So how are things going?" Dierdra asked.

It had been a while since they'd seen each other and even though they had made up, they hadn't really had the chance to spend time together since Kristen started working again.

"Pretty good," Kristen replied. "Work is going well and the kids are really well behaved."

"Caleb warming up a bit?"

"A little."

They were driving to Kristen's physical therapy appointment. They pulled up to the center and entered the lobby. Once she was checked in and waiting, Dede picked up her line of questioning again.

"How are things with Mark?"

Kristen nodded and smiled. "Really good, actually."

She thought about how patient he was, not pushing them to be anything more than what they were. He was consistently kind and attentive, always willing to help her and make her life easier. She thought back to the night he hugged her, after coming back from his therapist. She didn't know what they had discussed but he seemed more confident around her. He expressed himself without hesitation and allowed her to do the same, creating a trust that she needed in order to feel more comfortable around him.

"He kissed me," she whispered. Dede's eyes expanded like saucers. "When?"

"A while back." He hadn't tried it since then but sometimes Kristen wished he would. Though she would never admit it, there were plenty of nights when she wished she could take advantage of her marital status. What was the fun of being married if you couldn't make love to your spouse? She didn't know exactly what was holding her back but something told her that in order to be physically intimate with her husband, she needed to be emotionally intimate with him too.

"What's it going to take?" Dede asked, almost as if reading her mind.

"For what?" Kristen pretended ignorance.

Dede rolled her eyes. "Oh, come on, girl. Mark is a good man and a patient one too. But he *is* a man and he does have needs."

"And I don't?" she retorted.

"Okay, then! You've been back for two months now. Get it poppin'."

"Kristen! Good to see you." Jack emerged from the back and greeted her with a wide smile. Kristen stood up in relief, happy to table the conversation. She shook Jack' hand and introduced him to Dierdra. Though he greeted Dierdra warmly, Kristen noticed his smile falter just the slightest when he realized she was joining their appointment. For the past several weeks, Kristen had been seeing him alone. It also didn't escape her that while Dierdra shook his hand, she gave him a rather cool greeting.

The appointment was routine and once again, Jack made note of her improved balance and dexterity.

"How are the headaches doing?"

"A bit better," Kristen replied. "I use that stress ball whenever I'm overwhelmed and the breathing exercises you taught me. It helps prevent episodes more than treat them."

He nodded and gave her another mega watt smile. "'Prevention is better than cure,' right?"

Kristen glanced at Dede, who had remained noticeably quiet the entire appointment. She held a slight frown on her face but kept her silence.

"Well, keep up the good work. We're going to take you down to one appointment per week now. If you stay on track…"

"I'll be free at last."

He laughed and nodded. "You really can't stand me, can you?"

Kristen caught Dede rolling her eyes.

She's the one who can't stand you.

The minute they climbed in the car, Dierdra told her why.

"He likes you," she said assertively.

"Yeah, he's friendly to me."

"No, he *likes* you, Kristen," she repeated emphatically. "He flirted with you the entire session and practically undressed you with his eyes when you weren't looking."

"Why would he purposefully flirt with me? He knows I'm married."

"He also knows you don't remember the marriage. 'You can't stand me, can you?' What the hell was that? If he's like any one of those dogs out there, they don't care if you're married. If they like you, they'll try to holla."

"Well, I'm not hollering back."

"Mark loves you, Krissy."

"I know that," she replied, suddenly feeling defensive.

"Then you should-" Dierdra stopped herself. "Just be careful, Kristen."

"Mark, I'm home!" Kristen yelled out as she entered the house. The kids were still at school and wouldn't return for another hour and a half. She waited to hear his response but heard nothing. It was strange because his car was in the garage and he normally met her at the foyer as soon as he heard her voice. She went to his office, thinking he was engrossed in his work.

No sign of him.

She checked the family room, basement, and backyard - no luck.

Finally, she went upstairs and was surprised to find the bedroom door closed. She gently knocked and cracked it open, almost afraid of what she would find. Dierdra's voice came flooding back to her immediately.

"Mark is a good man and a patient one too. But he is a man and he does have needs."

"Mark?"

She stepped into the room and found all of the curtains drawn across the windows, casting the entire room in darkness. A trembling form lay under the sheets of the massive king sized bed. Kristen quietly approached the bed and found her husband laying there, fast asleep.

In all her months of living with them, she had *never* seen him take a nap. She tried to pull back the cover, but his fingers were clinging to it, wrapping it around his body as he shivered in his sleep.

The room wasn't cold.

On impulse, as if a maternal pull took hold of her, Kristen reached out and placed her hand on his forehead, his dark brown hair brushing the back of her hand. His skin was scorching hot and she didn't need a thermometer to know he had a really high fever. She walked into the bathroom, pulled a wash cloth and ran cool water on it. She returned with the damp cloth and folded it over his forehead. He stirred, frowned in discomfort and slowly opened his eyes. For a second he looked as if he didn't recognize her but then he remembered himself and tried to sit up, the cover slipping.

"Hi," he rasped out. His voice was scratchy and even lower in octave. Even though he was clearly sick, the sound of his rough timbre caused her belly to tighten in arousal. It didn't escape her that he was shirtless, the sweat of his fever glistening on his tight, taut muscles. She pushed the feeling of attraction aside and gently wiped his forehead with the cloth, pushing his shoulders back down as his head fell back against the pillow. He turned to look at the nightstand and wiped a hand over his face. Her eyes followed his gaze to the clock and she could almost read his thoughts aloud.

"Don't worry about the kids," she said immediately. "You need to rest. When did you start feeling like this?"

He cleared his throat but his voice was still scratchy.

"Last night. I thought it would go away but it's only gotten worse."

"How long have you been asleep?"

She could barely make out his blush in the dark room.

"Since this morning, after I dropped them off." She could see him stretch his long body under the covers as he yawned. "I've never slept so long."

"Did you have anything to eat?"

He shook his head. "Too tired."

She frowned in concern. She hated the thought of him being so sick and tired that he went without food all day. There was no thought and no hesitation. Kristen immediately took charge. She found the thermometer in their medicine cabinet, took his temperature and determined that he had some sort of flu. She called his doctor and set up an appointment for the next day but followed his orders in the interim.

She fixed Mark two large sandwiches, a bowl of soup, tea, and several bottles of water, insisting that he finish the entire fare in front of her. She propped him up against several stacked pillows at the headboard and tried to ignore his shirtless torso as he ate. In his weakened state, it took him a while to get through the sandwiches and by the time she gave him the warm soup, she was spoon feeding him despite his protests. She gave him NyQuil for his symptoms and ordered him to stay in bed.

"Thank you," he whispered weakly as he dozed off once again.

When the kids got home, she briefed them on their dad's condition and told them in no uncertain terms to leave him alone and stay away from his room. She was concerned that they would not only keep him from resting but that they too would catch whatever it was he had and the last thing she needed was a houseful of sick children *and* a sick husband. With Jasmine's help, Kristen prepared all of them dinner and helped out with Kylie and Caleb's homework. She was particularly glad to see that Caleb's assignment revolved around the history of journalism. To her astonishment, her name was listed on the sheet under the question: "Who was the first African American woman to anchor ABC *World News*?" It was still hard for her to believe that she was a public figure. She didn't feel like one most days, especially living in Georgia but she was one - one who even made history. Her son was coy the entire time he filled out the worksheet but she didn't miss the small smile he gave when he boldly circled her name from the answer choices.

That evening, Kristen learned exactly who was responsible for dishes and chores. She learned that all three kids, even Kylie, knew how to brush their teeth, shower, prepare for bed, and tuck themselves in without any assistance. Jasmine told her it was one of the things she had insisted they learn how to do from the time they were toddlers. Kylie still required a bedtime story and prayer each night but for the most part getting them settled into bed wasn't much of a challenge. It was a testament to the fact that she and Mark raised three very obedient and respectful children, who didn't take advantage of their father's illness.

"Mommy, can we pray for Daddy?"

Kristen smiled into her youngest daughter's eyes and couldn't help but feel a surge of longing to remember her infancy. She was absolutely precious at five-years-old. What was she like as a toddler and baby? She wondered the same about Caleb and even Jasmine as a young child. It suddenly bothered her that she *couldn't* remember carrying her children. And she couldn't remember making the decision to have them. That she couldn't remember what it felt like to grow her family and see it expand with her husband. She felt it tug at her heart but she pushed the thought away.

"Of course we can, sweetie."

She listened to Kylie's sweet little voice pray for her father's recovery. She couldn't help but observe how thoughtful the small child was. Not only did she ask that Mark get well but she prayed that he was comfortable in the process. That he would be able to sleep well and relax about the house running smoothly. The little girl knew her father well and prayed accordingly.

By the time Kristen emerged from Kylie's room, Jasmine and Caleb were both fast asleep. She was exhausted herself but needed to check on Mark. She made her way through the pitch black room and managed to find the lamp. She flicked it on and immediately regretted it as she watched

Mark grimace at the sudden light next to him. He shuddered awake and looked at her with bleary brown eyes.

"How you doing?" she whispered.

"Head hurts," he croaked back. He then started to cough. She gave him some more water and served him another dose of NyQuil. He scrunched his nose at the horrible taste before leaning back into the pillow and closing his eyes, his brows still stitched in a frown. She leaned forward and took hold of both his temples, massaging them. He froze at her touch, opening his eyes to meet hers.

"Relax," she said softly.

"Why are you doing this?" he asked. She knew what he meant. By helping him with the kids and nursing him with food and NyQuil, she could always say she was just doing what needed to be done. But in this moment, massaging his temples and touching him in a more intimate way than she had ever initiated before, they both knew something was shifting. Amid the NyQuil fog, he still managed to hold her eyes.

"Because I care," she replied. She didn't dare say she felt more than that. "You said your head is hurting and I don't want you to be in pain. So just relax. This should ease the tension."

She continued to rub and watched as he slowly closed his eyes, the tension between his brows disappearing and his breathing evening out. Before she knew it, he fell asleep, his cheek relaxing into her palm.

"Good morning."

Kristen eased her way into the room, confidently balancing the tray piled with eggs, sausage, oatmeal, fruit, orange juice, green tea, and DayQuil for her husband. Mark sat up in the bed with a grateful smile. Five-o-clock shadow covered his angular jaw and gave his handsome face an even more distinguished look. His eyes teased her as she crossed the room towards him.

"I don't know how you managed to get all of that onto one tray."

She settled the tray onto his lap, noticing with disappointment that he had pulled on a shirt while she was away. He looked better than he had last night. His eyes were more alert and he had more color in his cheeks. But his nose was still red and the tissues were piled high in the trash can parked next to the bed.

He took the DayQuil without complaint and dug into his breakfast. He glanced at her as she watched him eat.

"You didn't have to bring this up," he said around his food. "Thank you."

She shrugged. "My pleasure."

Surprisingly, it was. She enjoyed looking after him, taking over his responsibilities for a while. Making the kids breakfast and getting them ready for school really made her feel like a mom for the first time since her return.

Did I used to do that? Was that my life prior to the accident?

She didn't mind it. And Jasmine and Kylie seemed to enjoy it as well. Caleb was quiet and reserved as usual but he never questioned her authority or gave her a hard time as she filled his father's shoes. That particular morning, he looked like he had a lot on his mind. She wondered if it was because of that teacher of his.

When she shook herself out of her thoughts and refocused on Mark, he was already done with his breakfast and was watching her silently. She smiled at him, embarrassed for having zoned out. He smiled back, curious as to what was on her mind. She looked around and for the first time since her first night back, took a long look around their master suite. It really was a regal room, fit for the king and queen of the house. The bed itself was enormous.

Plenty of room for lovemaking.

The thought came out of nowhere and Kristen could feel heat rise to her face. She could still feel Mark's eyes on her but couldn't meet them at the moment. Once again, he was much more perceptive than she gave him credit for.

"Hard to believe you once slept here?"

She nodded.

"What about it is difficult?"

She shrugged and stammered, "We're married. We have three kids. Obviously we…we…"

"Made love."

She nodded again, silent for a moment. He watched and waited as she struggled for words. Finally she met his eyes, feeling steadied by the calmness in them.

"Did we wait?" she asked. "Until marriage?"

He nodded solemnly. "We did."

A feeling of relief washed over her but it didn't last for long. His eyes bore into hers and she felt a sense of panic all over again. This was the closest they'd come to discussing intimacy in weeks and though she desired him, she felt scared to take that first step.

What am I thinking bringing this subject up?

She quickly stood up, piled the dishes back on the tray and headed for the door.

"Kristen…"

"Your appointment is in an hour." she said over her shoulder. "You might want to shower before we head out."

Mark sighed as he got ready to go. He wished they could have tackled the question of sex that morning but he didn't really see how. Short of doing it, what was there to talk about? While he missed her and wanted to be with her again, it clearly made her uncomfortable to think about them being intimate in any fashion so he pushed it away and got ready.

Focus on the good.

There was a lot of good to focus on. Even though he still felt feverish and his congestion was out of control, he marveled at the way Kristen stepped up and took care of the kids without any problems. She was acting as the primary parent and nursing him all at the same time. Even more comforting was the fact that she seemed to enjoy serving him as his wife, setting her own needs aside to look after him. It was what she would have done prior to the accident and it gave him hope.

When they checked in at the doctor's office, it suddenly occurred to him that their visit was running into her recording time at the studio.

"Don't you have to be at work?" he asked her.

"I canceled," she replied. "They'll have one of the other anchors fill in for me tonight."

"Thank you," Mark said in astonishment. He knew it was a big deal for her to take time off, especially when she was trying to re-establish her presence as a leading anchor.

"You're welcome. I'm glad to."

He met her eyes and he knew she was being sincere. He loved her all the more.

"Mr. Tyverson?" the nurse called. "We're ready for you."

The appointment was short and straightforward. Mark and Kristen sat in the patient room as Dr. Turner, an old physician in his late sixties, examined him. As Kristen had estimated earlier, Mark did indeed have the flu.

"How did I get it?" he asked.

"Probably from one of your kids," his doctor replied. "School children are walking incubators of their classmates' germs."

"But none of them are sick." Kristen pointed out.

Mark rubbed his nose, his sinus clearly bothering him. "They all had their flu shots before Christmas break. You insisted before you left for Afghanistan."

"But you didn't get one?" she asked.

He shook his head. "I was going to do it the week after you got home but then…"

"I'm sorry," Kristen muttered.

"Why? It's not your fault. I'm the idiot who didn't plan ahead."

"You're not an idiot, Mark." Doctor Turner surmised. "You're just a busy father who got sidetracked with a lot of things." He gave him a warm smile, patted his shoulder, and handed him a piece of paper.

"This is a prescription for Tamiflu. Make sure you take it twice a day with meals for ten days. Your flu should run its course in ten to fourteen days."

Armed with medicine from the doctor and a sheaf of instructions from the clinic, Kristen returned home, determined to protect the kids from Mark's infection. She immediately placed him in bed, served him more food and ensured that he took his medicine. She deemed the master suite "the sick room." And informed their kids that beyond saying hello to their father through the door, they could not go in and he could not go out. She tasked Jasmine with making sure that no one, especially five-year-old Kylie, entered the room.

When she wasn't taking care of Mark or the kids, she was busy keeping the house clean and ensuring that everyone washed their hands, dishes, and linen on a regular basis. She saturated her body with Vitamin C and Zinc to protect her own immune system and at Mark's insistence, always wore a mask whenever she entered the room to check on him. With her care, the doctor's medicine, and his rest, Mark began to visibly improve by day five. Kristen reluctantly returned to work but limited her studio time to shooting - no research and no New York meetings. The show had to go on but she wouldn't put all of her time into it until things at home were in order.

As she had come to expect, the kids handled the whole situation very well. They all understood the severity of the flu and were careful to clean after themselves and avoid "the sick room" at all costs. After checking on Mark and cleaning her hands, Kristen walked into the kitchen to find her son poring over his school papers.

"Caleb, I thought you had finished your homework?" she asked.

"I did," he said quietly, refusing to look up.

She walked over to the table and looked down at the sheet in his hands. It was a writing assignment with the letter "C-" written in bold, red ink. Her heart sank as she noticed the other papers fanned out on the table with "C-," "B," and only one "A-" in sight. She looked back down at the sheet in his small, butterscotch hands.

"Wait a minute…"

She gently took the sheet from him.

"I recognize this…Didn't we do this one together?" She looked down at him as he nodded, a sour expression coloring his eyes. It was the journalism assignment they had gone over together. While the multiple choice answers were all marked as correct, the short answers that she and her son had crafted together were deducted several times over.

She picked up the other sheets on the table and flipped through them one by one. She noticed a pattern. If the answers were clear-cut and could be verified by an external source, Caleb aced the question hands down. But when it involved a short answer or any amount of subjectivity, he immediately lost points. She slowly began to read over his short answers and writing assignments, checking against the instructions to make sure he answered each question adequately. Kristen refused to allow bias to cloud her perspective. She refused to factor in his age and merely asked herself: *Does his response answer the question?* And though he could make small improvements here and there, by and large Caleb provided well-thought out answers that more than covered the scope of the question.

She then looked to the margin of his assignments. Perhaps Ms. Walker left notes on why she deducted points. There were none. Kristen frowned, the hairs standing on the back of her neck.

What does she want from him?

She took the sheaf of assignments and quickly sat at the family computer. She could feel her son's eyes watching her curiously as she pulled up the school website, went to the directory and looked up the teacher's email address. She logged into her personal account and quickly typed her a letter:

```
Dear Ms. Walker,

My name is Kristen Tyverson and I am Caleb
Tyverson's mother. I'm contacting you in regards to
my son's scores in your class. I have personally
reviewed his graded assignments and am concerned
about his writing and how he is measuring up in
```

your class. You recently issued him an assignment
on the history of journalism that he and I
completed together. I have my Bachelor and Master
degrees in Journalism and was surprised to find
that he missed so many points on the short answers
we worked on together. I would like to know what he
can do to improve his writing and better meet your
expectations for his assignments. Can we please
arrange a time to meet? I look forward to hearing
from you soon. Thank you for your time.

Sincerely,
Kristen Tyverson

She read it over, clicked send, and prayed that, that was all that was needed to turn things around. She looked back at her son, who was watching her with curious, sad eyes. She stood up, went over to him, and wrapped a hand around his small shoulder.

"You're a great student, Caleb. We'll figure this out."

"I feel so much better. You know, you really make a great nurse, Kristen." Mark teased as he watched his wife type away at her laptop. She paused and rolled her eyes. Mark's congestion had cleared and his fever was long gone by day fourteen. After a follow up with Dr. Turner, he was given the clear to "rejoin" the family.

"I'm glad you feel better," Kristen replied. "Now I can actually get back to the gym. I'm so behind on my workouts."

"How are you going to catch up?" he asked in an eerily quiet tone.

"I'm thinking if I leave at three for the next two weeks-"

"Three *AM*? Are you crazy?" he exclaimed.

She looked up at him and frowned. "Only for two weeks! Just to make up for-"

"For what? Giving your body a much-needed break? Kristen, you do know that you can destroy your body if you work out for too long? The muscles begin to tear and degrade instead of strengthening."

"That's for extreme people." She looked back at her laptop.

"I know. I'm looking at one," he retorted. Her head snapped back up. She could almost feel herself wither under the challenge in his eyes but she held them all the same.

"Hi Mommy, hi Daddy!" Kylie's little voice carried through the house as she and the other kids made their way in.

"Hey, sweetie! How was your day?" Mark asked. He dropped his intense scrutiny and turned to their youngest as she ran into the kitchen, his arms extended for a hug. Kristen pushed his comments away to the best of her ability.

As Kylie and Jasmine chatted away, she sat at the island, her laptop propped open while she did some research for a segment her show was doing. She looked up in time to see Caleb walk in, his shoulders stooped and his head low. Mark noticed too and frowned in concern.

"Hey buddy, how was your day?" he called out.

Caleb didn't answer. Mark glanced at Kristen and she stood up, following her son to the dining table as he shrugged off his backpack and pulled out his folder.

"What happened?" she asked softly.

He opened the folder and showed her his test score.

Another "C-" in bold red ink. Kristen quickly scanned the test and once again, it was the short answers and essay questions that were lowering his score.

"That little..." Kristen caught herself and marched back to her laptop, her eyes blazing. Mark frowned at his wife's reaction.

"What is it?" he asked.

"She nailed him again. Even after I emailed her and asked about how he can improve."

"You emailed her?" Caleb asked.

She nodded and turned to Mark. "I asked her what he can be doing to better meet her expectations on his written answers. She never responded. She allowed him to take another test without giving any feedback as to how he can improve. I'm going to call her."

"No!" Caleb exclaimed. Kristen turned to him and frowned.

"Why not?"

"Just wait a minute," Mark began.

"Why?" Kristen snapped back. "We've been waiting for *months* now and this hasn't gotten any better."

"Bartholomew Academy is the best private school in the state of Georgia. We don't want to ruffle too many feathers unnecessarily."

She frowned again and he knew that was the last thing she wanted to hear. But how could he explain to her how hard they had worked to get all three of their kids into that school? How many doors it would open if they all successfully graduated from the academy? He didn't want to risk retaliation from the very strict school board.

"If this teacher isn't doing her job, she needs to be held accountable."

"But we don't know that she's not doing her job. It might just be a miscommunication."

Kristen sighed. "I don't understand why we can't just address this issue directly."

"What does it matter to you?" a surly little voice grumbled. All eyes turned to Caleb as he glared down at his folder, his little hands curled into tight fists.

"What did you say?" Mark challenged, in a stern, foreboding voice. Jasmine and Kylie exchanged a look and focused their attention back on Caleb.

"What does it matter to you?" Caleb repeated, louder, raising his glare to Kristen's face. She frowned in surprise. Why was he mad at her? Wasn't she just trying to help? For a minute, Kristen had actually started to believe that she and Caleb were developing an understanding; that this grade fiasco was a means of bringing them closer together.

Clearly I was wrong, she thought.

"Caleb, it matters to me because you matter to me," she said calmly.

"No, I don't!" he snapped back, his eyes beginning to water. "You care about Jasmine and Kylie and you like my dad again but you don't give a shit about me!"

Kristen and the girls gasped at his language.

"Caleb Tyverson - that is enough!" Mark's voice thundered through the kitchen. The whole room went silent. A look of outrage filled his face and Kristen knew he was restraining himself from fully expressing it.

"Caleb, go to your room," Kristen said quietly.

The boy quickly packed his things, took his snack, and silently retreated to his room. The girls, unsure of what to say, slipped into the family room and got started on their homework. Mark rubbed a hand over his face and sighed out his frustration. His son deserved to be rebuked and he was glad he did it in that moment. At the same time, though, he didn't want his son to think he was unloved or ignored. He knew he had to talk to him again. He looked over at Kristen.

She was staring at her laptop but not writing anything, her mind clearly on what had just taken place. She was clearly hurt by Caleb's outburst. He walked around the island and settled down beside her.

"I'm sorry," he said.

She smiled tremulously as he pulled her into his arms.

⌒✺〇

"I'm worried about Caleb," Mark said without preamble.

Dr. Longinow frowned. "What's going on with him?"

"What isn't going on with him? He's not improving in school. His grades are still slipping. He's not adjusting to Kristen like the girls are. Every time I see them with her, they've grown even closer, almost like old times."

"But with him…?"

"With him, it's the opposite. He's withdrawn and cantankerous. On a good day, he just ignores her."

He told her about the recent fight.

"He was so nasty to her. Just when we thought things were getting better, he explodes at her. I've talked with him about it before but he's not getting any better."

"How is Kristen responding to this?"

Mark looked at his favorite place in the room, the pattern on the lamp shade beside the doctor.

"She's patient with him. Cordial and polite - even when he's rude to her, she handles it without snapping."

"But how is *she* responding to it?"

Understanding the question, Mark continued, "She won't admit it, but I know it hurts her. She doesn't know what she did to this child for him to be so mean to her. And she doesn't know what to do to rectify it. Even worse, just as she's starting to feel more comfortable back home, he'll say or do something that sets her back several steps. In those moments, I can tell she once again feels like a guest at a hotel, not a wife and mother in her own home."

Dr. Longinow's frown had since deepened and Mark could see she was very concerned.

"This can't go on much longer," she said. "Bring them in next week."

"What?"

"You heard me. Bring Caleb and Kristen in next week and I'll talk to them."

Mark shook his head. "Kristen won't come in."

"She will if it involves helping Caleb. Bring them in."

"I'm telling you, she won't do it."

One Week Later

"Kristen, Caleb, I'm so glad you two could make it today. Thank you for agreeing to see me."

Caleb kept quiet. Kristen nodded and smiled stiffly.

Mark leaned back in his seat and watched the interaction play out. He had done his part and could only hope for the best. After days of entreating and pleading with his wife to help him take Caleb in, she finally relented for "just this session."

Kristen observed Dr. Longinow silently. She was a beautiful woman in her mid-thirties with long, wavy blonde hair and kind hazel eyes. She glanced at Mark and it occurred to Kristen that he'd been spending a lot of time in therapy with her. She felt an irrational surge of dislike for the woman and trusted her even less.

"Mark, Kristen, can I ask you to give Caleb and me some time alone?"

They acquiesced and stepped out into the waiting room. Mark glanced back at his son's nervous eyes and gave him a reassuring smile.

"We'll be back soon," he said before the therapist closed the door.

He joined Kristen in the lobby and noticed that she was markedly quiet, staring off into space as opposed to reading a magazine or book like she normally would.

"You okay?"

"I'm fine," she curtly replied, refusing to meet his eyes.

"What do you think of Dr. Longinow?" he asked, searching for small talk.

"I just met her," she reminded him. After a pause, she added, "*You* seem to like her."

What does that *mean?* he thought.

He looked at her and waited until she met his eyes. She did, briefly, and then looked back forward.

"She's very pretty," she said.

He was astonished.

She's jealous!

While a part of him soared at knowing that she cared about his affection and fidelity, another part of him needed to nip her doubts in the bud immediately.

"Kristen, she's my therapist. *Our* therapist, hopefully."

She ignored the suggestion and kept her eyes forward.

"I've never been interested in her." He caught her chin and turned her head to face him. "I love *you*."

They held each other's gaze for a long moment. He could see the very moment she chose to believe him. Her face relaxed and a hint of a smile touched the corner of her lips.

"Even if you were...interested-"

"I'm not."

"Even if you were," she repeated. "I don't know why it should matter to me."

"Yes, you do." he softly challenged.

She searched his eyes.

"I'm your husband. You're my wife. You know why it matters."

"Mark? Kristen? You can come in now." Dr. Longinow called.

They walked back into the room and found Caleb staring at his hands on the couch.

"Okay," she said as they settled back into their seats. "Caleb gave me some insight as to how he's doing and he wanted to say something to you both."

Both parents turned to the child in between them and watched as he kept his gaze lowered. He was silent for a few long moments but finally began to speak.

"I feel left out," he mumbled. "Everyone likes the girls but I don't fit in."

"Have you always felt this way, Caleb?" Dr. Longinow asked.

He shook his head.

"When did it start?"

He mumbled something incoherently.

"Say it louder, sweetie. Just like you told me earlier."

He raised his head and met Kristen's eyes.

"It started when you came back."

"Caleb-" Mark began but stopped himself at Dr. Longinow's raised hand.

"Go ahead, Caleb, finish what you were telling me."

Caleb sighed and twisted his small fingers.

"You were supposed to come back. You promised," his voice began to tremble. "But when you didn't, I knew it wasn't your fault; that you were with God. But then you did come back and I was happy until - until..."

"Until...?" Kristen asked anxiously, her focus entirely on him.

"Until you said 'Who *are* these people?'" he exclaimed, quoting her verbatim. "Like we had a disease or something."

Kristen's eyes widened in shock. It had never even occurred to her that, that moment on the lawn had hurt him so deeply. But the more she thought about it, she could pinpoint it as the moment that shifted Caleb from being happy to see her to being completely cold towards her.

She could see why.

Caleb continued, "You said, 'Where is my family?' You forgot about us. But it didn't matter to Dad or Kylie or Jasmine because you were 'back.'" He hooked his fingers into quotation marks. "And now I'm the jerk for minding. I'm the party pooper for wanting my mom back. The mom who knows me. I don't know you and you don't care."

"But I do care-"

"Are you hearing that, Caleb?" Dr. Longinow stepped in. "What did your mother just say?"

"That she cares," he muttered.

"That she what?"

"That she cares," he repeated louder.

"Why don't you believe her?"

He shrugged.

"Why don't you believe her?" she repeated again, unfazed. Kristen looked at the therapist and was impressed with her tenacity.

"She doesn't know me." Caleb talked to his hands. "And she doesn't want to."

"Of course I want to," Kristen said. "You're my son. I love you."

His head snapped up and searched her eyes. She met his unwaveringly and felt a sense of relief in finally articulating what had been on her heart for weeks.

"Caleb, it's true." she assured him. "I don't remember having you or Kylie or Jasmine-"

"You adopted her."

"You know what I mean," she smiled. "I don't remember having any of you or even marrying your dad but I love you. You're my family and I don't need to remember everything to love you all again."

Mark looked on in astonishment and watched as Kristen opened her heart to their son, fearlessly risking his rejection. Her words were candid and tender and grew the already expanding hope in his own heart. She loved their kids again. She loved them.

Does this mean she can love me too?

He refocused his attention on them.

"I'm sorry that I hurt you before, Caleb. I didn't want for any of this to happen. But I do love you and I am glad to be back. I want us to be closer if you're willing to give us a chance."

"You're not mad at me?" he asked in a voice so quiet, she almost didn't catch the question.

"I never have been," she replied.

Those were the magic words. No sooner had they left her mouth when Kristen started to feel his small arms wrap around her waist, his head burying into her chest as silent tears escaped his eyes. She held him tightly and kissed the top of his curly head, her heart soaring at the one-eighty that just happened.

"I'm sorry," he cried into her blouse.

"It's okay," she whispered back. "You didn't mean it."

She raised her eyes and caught Mark beaming at her, his own tears held in check. After a few moments, mother and son calmed down. Dr. Longinow passed them both tissues and met Caleb's eyes.

"I am *so* proud of you. This is just the start of a really good thing, okay?"

"Okay."

The session over, they all stood to leave.

"Kristen, could I have a word?" she asked. Kristen hung back while the two guys headed for the lobby. She met the younger woman's hazel eyes and waited.

"It was really nice to see you. I think after today you would agree that therapy can help."

Kristen nodded silently, not liking where the conversation was headed. Dr. Longinow went there anyway.

"Please come back with Mark."

Wow! She had a way of getting straight to the point.

Before she could protest, Dr. Longinow added, "I won't push you beyond what you allow and I can assure you that I *am* trustworthy."

Kristen frowned at the emphasis. *Does she...?* Kristen shook it off. She couldn't possibly know.

"Please. Mark needs your support in this and it can do wonders for your adjustment. Please come back."

"I'll think about it," Kristen replied distractedly.

"Thank you."

<hr>

"Are you attracted to him?" Dr. Longinow asked.

Kristen blinked and felt her face get hot. Against her better judgment, she had agreed to see her again with Mark. This time, the therapeutic spotlight was hot on her and she was already beginning to regret coming.

To Mark's surprise, she nodded in answer to the question. "I find it hard to concentrate when he's in the same room."

She refused to meet Mark's intense scrutiny. She would have seen him smiling in wonder. Dr. Longinow was also smiling.

"I want you guys to do an exercise here and now."

The couple looked at her questioningly.

"Turn and face each other."

They did as she said and shifted their positions. Immediately, Kristen found it difficult to meet Mark's eyes but his devoured her like a starving man. She could only meet his eyes for a couple seconds before turning to see Dr. Longinow observing her.

"Kristen, Mark loves to look at you. His eyes rest on you every few seconds and it's the result of being completely comfortable in your presence because he knows you intimately. You used to do the very same thing prior to your accident."

Kristen raised an eyebrow in surprise.

"I want you two to do an exercise where you look into one another's eyes uninterrupted for one minute."

Kristen frowned in panic. She felt Mark's hand reach out to hold her own. She looked back at him and saw him smile reassuringly.

"It's okay," he said. "I won't bite."

This is ridiculous. He's my husband - I should be able to look him in the eye. And yet she still felt nervous. There was something about holding a person's gaze for any extended period of time. What would she find when she looked? She already knew the answer. She had met his eyes many times before and they had always held the same emotion: love. The question was, what would he find?

Just get it over with.

Kristen took a deep breath, glanced at Dr. Longinow and finally settled on Mark's kind and patient brown eyes.

"One minute," the doctor repeated softly.

Mark felt his wife's hand tense at the reminder. Her eyes were guarded, almost scared and he wondered if she thought he was judging her. Her expression was almost pained at having to do this exercise and he wanted to put her at ease. The doctor beat him to it.

"How are you feeling, Kristen?" she asked.

"Keep looking?" she asked, as if they were in class and Dr. Longinow was the teacher.

"Yes, Kristen, keep looking but let me talk you through this. How are you feeling?"

Mark looked at her expectantly and saw a shift in her expression.

"Uncomfortable," she finally answered. Her eyes started to tear and Mark squeezed her hand slightly, trying to comfort her as the doctor did her thing.

"Why is this uncomfortable for you?"

"Because I don't *know* him." She immediately saw a glimpse of sadness in his eyes, though he tried his best to hide it.

"Are you sure about that?" Dr. Longinow asked.

"What do you mean?"

"You have been living with Mark and your children for a few months now. What have you observed about him as a person so far?"

Kristen took a deep breath again and started to speak.

"He's kind-"

"Tell him, Kristen. Speak to him. He's right in front of you."

Kristen stopped and tried to collect her thoughts as she looked into Mark's waiting eyes.

"You're patient," she blurted out. "You're kind. You put others before yourself all the time and just when I think you're a pushover, you prove yourself to be a great leader, an assertive man."

She saw the surprise in his eyes which soon turned into tenderness as she continued to speak, "You have a rare, quiet confidence that doesn't require you to posture. You're a real man. A good man. A great one."

The more she spoke, the more she caved. Her defenses went down and she felt as if she were falling headlong into the pools of his eyes. As if they were connecting souls. She couldn't take it anymore. Kristen looked down and tried to pull her hand away but Mark held it fast.

"Look at me," he commanded. She shook her head and tried to turn to the therapist. Mark caught her legs with his free hand and gently shifted her back to face him.

"Look at me," he repeated more fervently. She raised her eyes and was surprised to find an expression of sheer joy on his face. He held one of her hands firmly but used his other hand to caress her cheek.

"I love you," he said, voice deepening with emotion. "If this is how you view me, why is it so hard for you to let me love you?"

"It's not hard," she whispered back. "I make it hard but only because I have to."

"Why, Kristen?" Dr. Longinow asked.

Kristen looked between the two of them. "Because this doesn't feel real. I feel like an impostor in someone else's life."

Understanding dawned on Mark.

Kristen continued, "The kids, the house, the assets. I don't remember working for any of this. I don't know how to be a good mom. I don't know what these kids are used to. It's a miracle I still even have a job!"

Mark's hand dropped from her cheek to her shoulder. He rubbed it in gentle circles, attempting to calm his wife. He glanced at Dr. Longinow, who was staring hard at her notes. She suddenly looked up and spoke to Kristen.

"Focus on you and Mark."

Once again, they looked at her questioningly.

"Focus on you and Mark. Focus on your marriage. In fact, don't even think of it as 'your marriage' but focus on your relationship with one another. Kristen, you've already discovered that you're still you for the most part. The career piece is fine and you're getting treated for your health. You're still attracted to your husband and he's still attracted to you. The next step is to re-acquaint yourself with your family. The gateway and foundation to that family is your relationship with Mark."

Kristen nodded. She knew that made sense but she almost wanted a dotted outline.

"How?" she asked simply.

"Go on dates," the therapist replied. She turned to Mark. "Pretend you're just meeting her again like you did all those years ago. Take her out and let her get to know you again."

Mark nodded, locked and loaded. "Okay."

Their first date was scheduled in a small restaurant on the edge of Atlanta. It was the strangest date Kristen had ever been on. For one thing, she needed a babysitter before going out. For another, her eldest daughter was serving as said babysitter. The last time Kristen had been on a date, it was Dierdra who had helped her get dressed. This time, her two daughters were filling that role. Both girls very decisive, they overruled several of Kristen's outfits before unanimously voting for her form fitting, little black dress; a sexy little number that fell just above her knees, scooped into a neckline at her decolletage and accentuated her slender curves. She wasn't sure it was a good choice until she faced him in the upstairs hall. He had gotten ready with Caleb's assistance. The minute she saw his face, Kristen knew she was giving Mark a run for his money. His eyes roved over her body in open appreciation and his Adam's apple bobbed up and down as he swallowed hard. He was dressed in a pair of black slacks and a crisp, white-collared shirt. His thick brown hair was tousled in a sexy pile atop his head. They met at the middle of the hall.

Captivated, he simply whispered, "Stunning."

"Thank you." She smiled. His eyes were all she could see and in that moment, she wanted nothing more than to be with him.

"What are you waiting for?" Caleb asked, snapping them into reality and ushering them to the door.

"Bye!" Jasmine said. "Have fun. But no more siblings, please."

Kristen felt heat rise to her face while Mark shot Jasmine a look. "Bed by nine. Understood?"

He grabbed his wife's hand and bid them all farewell.

When they pulled up to the restaurant, Kristen couldn't help but laugh in delight.

"Rosetta's." She turned and looked at his grinning face. They walked into the restaurant hand-in-hand and followed the maître d' to their reserved table. It was a beautiful, quiet setting with three small candles lit between them.

"When was the last time we ate here?" she asked.

"Our tenth anniversary. July 7, 2013." He watched her as she sipped her pink rosé, a curious expression on her face.

"You want to know what the wedding was like," he guessed. "It was beautiful. Just family and friends."

She looked up at him. "That is so creepy."

He frowned. "What is?"

"Your ability to read me - read my mind. It's like you know my thoughts before I even articulate them."

He smiled, relaxing. "After ten years, I think it's pretty much par for the course. Besides, you've never been good at hiding your thoughts. They just flash across your face as you think them."

She rolled her eyes at him as he laughed.

"Well, the whole point of this date is for me to get to know you better." She paused. "Tell me about your childhood."

His eyes lowered to his plate as he chewed his food.

He swallowed and said, "I was a military brat. My dad was a Marine and we lived in Japan, Nigeria, Thailand, Eastern Europe...all over, really."

"What did your mom do?"

"She was a missionary. As far as she was concerned, wherever we went was wherever she was called to minister. It worked out for both of them."

"Did you like it?" she asked, already knowing the answer.

He frowned. "Not really. I hated having to make friends all over again every two or three years. Having to constantly acquaint myself with a new town, much less a new country. It was exhausting."

"That's why you like stability," she surmised.

He smiled and nodded, searching her eyes.

"Are your parents still alive?"

His smile dimmed a bit.

"My dad is. Mom passed away when I was seventeen. Breast cancer."

"I'm so sorry." As hard as it was losing her mother, Kristen couldn't fathom losing her as a teen.

"How did you do it?"

He shrugged. "I just did. I had no other choice. Dad got over it pretty quickly though. He remarried less than a year later."

Kristen gasped. "Ouch."

He shrugged, a mixture of sadness and irritation in his eyes. He began to pick at his food, his mind clearly on other things.

"Do you have any siblings?" she asked.

He nodded. "Two brothers. I'm the oldest."

"You seem like it." He smiled at that.

"What was your mom like?" His fork paused and he set it down. He looked up at his wife and held her gaze for a long time.

"Gentle. Considerate. She was the sort of person who made you feel welcome in any circumstance. The warmest person I ever knew. She would have loved you."

Kristen frowned. "I'm not gentle or warm."

"You're strong and loving and honest. And you can be *very* gentle and warm. She would love you and see why I love you."

"I feel like I got the better end of the deal in this marriage."

"That's good because I feel the same way about you."

Her heart immediately skipped, touched by his words. He reached across the table and held her left hand, caressing the ring finger. It didn't escape her that she hadn't worn a wedding ring since her return. She didn't even know where it was. But she noticed that he still wore his and marveled at his integrity. They smiled at each other.

When they finished eating, Kristen thought they were done for the night but Mark insisted they weren't.

"I have a surprise for you."

Fifteen minutes later, they were stepping into the lobby of an upscale Hilton Hotel. Kristen looked at Mark in surprise; half excited, half terrified.

"What are we doing here?"

He frowned at her reaction and held out his hands reassuringly.

"Calm down. We're not getting a room."

She wasn't prepared for the sinking of her heart when he said that.

What is wrong with me? she thought. *Am I really that eager to sleep with him?*

But why not? another part of her reasoned. *He is your husband.*

Mark spoke in hushed tones with the receptionist at the front. Immediately, the staff member escorted them down the halls to what looked like a large banquet room. He handed Mark the keys to the double doors and excused himself. Mark unlocked the doors, reached for Kristen, and ushered her in the room, guiding her by the small of her back. She ignored the slight thrill of him touching her there and focused her attention on the room. To her astonishment, it was a theater room, equipped with several aisles of seats, cup holders, and a giant screen center stage.

They were the only two there.

"You planned this?" Kristen gasped.

"Mmm-hmm."

"*When?*" she asked in amazement.

"Don't worry about it," he replied. "Just enjoy it with me. It feels amazing to spend time with you - just the two of us."

She agreed. She turned to him and wrapped her arms around his neck, pulling him flush against her body. She noticed that he stiffened but ignored it and whispered, "Thank you."

It was such a thoughtful and intentional gesture. Yet another way he was showing her that she meant the world to him. She loved that about him. That he didn't just *say* he loved her but he found ways to show it all the time.

I'm falling for him.

Mark could feel his control slipping. First the dress, then the dinner, and now the hug. He could feel every curve of her body mold into his and his desire suffused his senses. *Get a hold of yourself!* He pulled back, took a deep breath, and escorted her to the center of the theater. He looked towards the projection room, raised his hand, and the film began to roll.

The first reel showed a beautiful, clear blue sky. Several shots captured details of the surroundings: lush green grass, tall oak trees, and beautiful, manicured flowers. The details grew more defined and Kristen began to recognize the setting: Raleigh Tavern, Bruton Parish Church, and…

"The Governor's Palace! This is Colonial Williamsburg!"

Mark smiled as he watched his wife absorb the film with curiosity. He wanted to see when it would finally register to her what she was watching. It did as soon as she saw the date appear on screen.

"July 7, 2003." She gasped as the screen cut to her in her wedding dress. She was stunning in a breathtaking strapless gown that cinched at her waist and fanned out into a full dress skirt, made entirely of tulle. She watched as Dierdra helped her with her gown and her other bridesmaids fawned over her hair. Tears sprang to her eyes as her mother re-arranged her veil on the screen.

The film cut to Mark getting ready and she noticed how much younger they both looked. Fresh-faced and excited before three kids and busy careers aged them to their late thirties.

We still look good, she thought, glancing at her husband beside her.

The ceremony took place on the lawn in front of The Governor's Palace. Kristen vaguely wondered how much money they spent on the ceremony. The entire park was closed off and they, along with their guests, were the only people present at the ceremony. She watched as they exchanged vows and she could feel Mark's eyes on her as she began to tear at the words they said. She saw the look of absolute adoration on her twenty-six-year-old face and she smiled in contentment.

Leaning into Mark, she enjoyed the warmth of his embrace as he whispered in her ear, "I would have sprung for *Titanic* but that's a little long."

She burst out laughing and he chuckled right beside her. Scenes from the reception played on as she re-focused her attention on her husband and said, "This was wonderful. Thank you for showing me this."

He met her eyes and smiled. "My pleasure. It was our beginning."

The ride home was quiet and comfortable. By the time they drove into the garage, it was almost midnight and both adults were tired, yet satisfied. Kristen couldn't stop smiling as she waited for Mark to open her side of the door. He offered her his hand as she climbed out and closed the door behind her. Just as she was about to make her way to the door, she felt his hands at her waist. He pulled her back, pinned her to the car, and kissed her squarely on the mouth.

Finally, she thought.

Her hands wrapped around his neck as she returned his kiss eagerly, her lips opening at the prodding of his tongue. He sucked her bottom lip into his mouth and she felt a spark go through her spine. She deeply inhaled his fresh, masculine cologne and enjoyed the feel of his hands tightly holding her waist. She stroked the back of his neck and played her fingers through his hair. All she could hear was their heavy breathing. Her hands made their way to the buttons on his shirt when he suddenly pulled back, face flush, a lock of hair falling into his eyes.

"I want you," he panted. His words shot another spike of pleasure through her and she moved closer to him. He stepped back.

"I want you," he repeated. "But I don't want to rush you. Are you sure you want to do this? Because if you aren't, tell me now while I can stop."

She did stop, clarity finally taking hold of her mind. What was she doing? He'd only kissed her and she was already all over him, ready to go at it.

Use your brain, Kristen.

She took a deep breath, calming down as he watched her.

"I want you too," she said softly. "But we're just getting to know each other again. So I want to take it slow. I had a really good time tonight."

He smiled. "Me too."

"Can I kiss you again?"

He looked at her in surprise but slowly nodded. He closed the distance between them, reached up and held her cheek. The kiss was softer, much gentler, deliberate and slow. She could feel him restraining himself for her sake. They pulled back, looked at each other and smiled.

Mission accomplished.

CHAPTER TEN
Mark's Family

"Kylie, come wish Savannah happy birthday." Mark called.

Kylie rushed into the kitchen and began to sing to her cousin. Kristen looked on in curiosity. Again, it occurred to her that Mark had an entire family of origin that she had no recollection of meeting. They had been making it a point to go on as many dates as possible, often during the day and sometimes during the weeknights when Jasmine had less homework and could watch the kids; but Mark didn't mention his side of the family on a regular basis.

Mark caught her watching Kylie on the phone and filled in some of the blanks.

"Savannah is our five-year-old niece. My brother's youngest daughter."

"Middle brother or youngest brother?"

He smiled. "Middle. Matthew."

She knew that there was Mark, Matthew, and Michael. His parents were fond of alliteration.

"Mommy, Savannah wants to say hi to you."

Mark frowned and looked at Kristen. She shrugged and took the phone from their daughter, watching as she skipped off into the family room.

"Hi, Savannah, happy birthday."

"Hi Kristen," a deep baritone voice answered. Kristen gasped. It sounded so much like Mark's she had to look over at him to make sure he hadn't spoken. Mark frowned at her reaction.

"Forgive me," the man continued. "But I was afraid I wouldn't get the chance to talk to you unless I did that. This is Matt, Savannah's dad. I'm Mark's younger brother."

"I know who you are." Kristen answered. She shook her head at Mark, who was mouthing "What?" in concern.

"Oh, good!" he responded, pleasantly surprised. The more he spoke, the more she noticed his southern accent. It was deeper and more defined than Mark's cultured dialect.

"Listen, I just wanted to make sure you knew about the invitation to the little family get-together this weekend."

"No, I didn't know." She frowned. What had Mark been keeping from her?

"Yeah, well we're celebrating Dad's sixty-fifth birthday this weekend and we were hoping to see you all, especially after your accident. We didn't want to overwhelm you but we do miss you so I hope y'all will come on down."

Kristen glared at Mark and calmly said, "Absolutely. We would love to see you all again and I can't think of a better way than to do it celebrating your father."

His eyes rounded like saucers. Mark knew that Savannah hadn't been on the phone for a while but he couldn't believe Matt had the gall to go around him and push them into an unwanted trip. He watched as his wife ended the call with his brother and turned to him with a hand on her hip.

"Why didn't you tell me?"

"Because I don't want to go."

"They're your family, Mark."

"I know that-"

"And it's your father's birthday."

"He has a birthday every year."

"I don't get it," she shook her head. "Family is so important to you. Why won't you-"

He stepped up to her and cut her off with, "*Our* family is important to me, Kristen. You don't know my side of the family. You don't know the things that have happened-"

"I would if you'd tell me."

"What? The same way you'd tell me about what happened to you?"

Her mouth dropped. She immediately closed it and pulled up a guarded expression.

"What are you talking about?"

He held her eyes and softened his expression. "I *know*, Kristen. I know about what happened to you."

She frowned. "No, you don't."

He looked around them and lowered his voice. "Your stepdad? The man your mom wanted to be buried next to but you refused? I know what he did to you. The things he said, the way he hurt you."

Tears sprung to her eyes and she shook her head. She felt an overwhelming desire to distance herself from him and she took several steps back, each one matched by his steps forward.

"Don't run away from me. I love you. You can trust me."

"How do you know?"

"You told me. Shortly before we got married. It took us a few years after that but we started seeing Dr. Longinow to help you get past it."

Understanding dawned on her. She remembered what Dr. Longinow had said about being trustworthy. She had known.

"Then you also know why I didn't want to see a therapist in the first place."

He nodded, a snarl of disgust shaping his lips. "The therapist you saw as a child should have his license revoked. What he did was unethical and dangerous. He broke your trust the minute he chose not to believe you."

"He said it wasn't really abuse. He said that words can't really hurt you. That as long as he didn't touch me-"

"That man tortured you and tried to make you believe that you weren't beautiful enough or thin enough or good enough. He tried to break you down and he did it because you refused to let him have what he never should have wanted to begin with."

She began to shake.

"You never told your mom. Just me. And then Dr. Longinow."

She folded her arms into her chest and looked down at them. "I wish I remembered the sessions. You said I had improved."

He nodded. "You did improve. And you can improve again. I'm with you."

She looked up and nodded. Mark hesitated and stepped forward again.

"Can I hold you?" he asked her. She nodded again and in a millisecond, Mark closed the distance between them and pulled her into his arms. She unfolded her own and wrapped them around his strong back, digging her face into his neck and inhaling his comforting scent.

Another wall had been torn.

The kids were thrilled to learn of their impromptu trip to Texas. They packed in record speed and gave Mark and Kristen no trouble at the airport and on the plane. She was seriously beginning to wonder how often she and Mark put the hammer down earlier in order to get such well-behaved kids. It was almost abnormal.

The flight was a short one - only three hours direct. The entire family stepped out of the terminal and headed to baggage claim, shocked to find a large group congregated by the claim area with their bags already collected.

"Surprise!" the group yelled out. "Welcome back, guys!"

The kids raced over to the throng of brown, blonde, and red-haired people: Mark's massive family. Mark took one look at his wife's face and knew she was already regretting her decision to come.

He found her hand and held it tightly, leaning down, he whispered, "I'm right here. Don't worry."

She looked up and smiled. "Ditto."

They slowly walked over to the convention and immediately felt arms pulling them into strong, warm hugs. Kristen could feel several small hands wrapped around her waist as the kids from the group yelled, "Auntie Kris! Auntie Kris!" There were far too many names and faces to remember but Kristen tried her best to remember the most important ones as they introduced themselves to her all over again.

"Kristen, you look wonderful!" a petite, red-headed woman exclaimed. She pulled her into a hug and quickly said, "I'm Tami, Matthew's wife and Savannah's mom."

She pointed at her husband, a tall, meaty man who looked like Mark with twenty extra pounds on him. He turned just in time to pull her into a hug and said, "I'm the one who tricked you. So glad you decided to come."

He pointed to the little blonde girl chattering away with Kylie. "That's Savannah there. And those two knuckle heads are Alex and Dawson, our twin boys."

Another man, the exact same height as Mark and Matt but with clear blue eyes and a thinner physique, approached Kristen as well. He leaned forward and kissed her cheek.

"I'm-"

"Michael?" Kristen guessed.

He laughed. "You're good. Yep, I'm Michael and this is my wife, Sienna."

The waifish blonde attached to his hip also kissed her cheek.

"Our boys are back at the house. You'll meet them then."

Oh great. There are more?

Between the luggage, children, and variety of cars, it took a while for the group to figure out how to get home. Mark insisted that he and his family pick up their rental car as planned. Tami put up a bit of a fight: "But we came all this way to pick you up!"

After a while though, reason won out and they all agreed to meet at the family house in an hour. That was one thing Mark couldn't get around. His father owned a massive ranch on the outskirts of Tyler, Texas and had more than enough room to house all three of his children *and* their families. While Mark hated the idea of being in close proximity to the *entire* family for more than a few hours, he knew better than to insult the patriarch of the family by renting a hotel.

Said patriarch was waiting on the front porch of his massive ranch home when he, Kristen, and the kids pulled up. Kristen looked around at the vast property in wonder.

How on earth can anyone maintain a property of this size?

They stood on at least five hundred acres worth of land. It looked like something out of an old Americana picture book; with sprawling green grass, rows of vegetation, bales of hay, and several livestock scattered about the terrain. The house was all timber, stacked atop each other in hand-made precision. The American flag flew proudly off the front porch and Kristen had no doubt that they were in Texas.

Mark glanced at his wife taking it all in, turned off the ignition, and stepped out of the car. His father met him halfway.

"Mark! Good to see you, son." Mason Tyverson gave his son a firm handshake and pulled him into a gruff hug. Mark's father was every inch the southern rancher if she could imagine one. He stood just two inches shorter than his son's six foot four. Though sixty-five, the man stood straight, had a head full of thick gray hair, and dark brown eyes that matched his son's. He was developing a bit of a belly but his legs were lean and his arms were strong. If Kristen weren't already aware of his age, she would have guessed him to be in his early to mid-fifties.

"Grandpa!"

The kids scrambled out of the car and raced to the older man as he crouched on his haunches and pulled them all into his arms. Kristen stepped out of the car and made her way to Mark's side. They found each other's hands and watched their kids serenade their grandfather. Kristen glanced up at Mark and saw the tense outline of his jaw.

"You alright?" she whispered.

He looked down at her and nodded. "Yeah." But she could see his eyes were troubled.

"Okay, okay, let me loose now. I want to say hello to your mother."

The kids raced off into the house and around the back yard, eager to find their cousins and continue playing.

Mason stood to his full height, once again towering over Kristen. He walked up to her and gently pulled her into his arms, forcing her to let go of Mark's hand.

"Welcome home, sweetheart," he whispered in a gentle timbre. Kristen returned the hug and felt that his scent reminded her of wood burning in a cozy fire. It was comforting and he seemed friendly.

"Thank you, Mr. Tyverson. It's good to be back."

"Oh nonsense," he waved his hand and grinned a warm smile. "Call me Mason or Dad - whatever you prefer."

He looked at his son, who stood to the side with a blank expression.

"How was the flight?"

Mark nodded and said in an even blanker tone, "Fine. Thanks for having us."

"Nonsense," he said again. "I want all the family around me on my birthday. I missed you guys," he said meaningfully. Mark ignored the meaning and headed to the car, busying himself with unloading the luggage. Kristen frowned. What happened to the caring, easygoing husband she was used to? She'd never seen Mark behave so coldly towards anyone before.

"Mark, you put those suitcases down this instant!" a bossy female voice called from the front porch. A tall, red-headed woman in her early forties barreled down the stairs, walked right past Kristen and Mason and continued straight to Mark, with her arms extended.

That's weird. Mark didn't mention anything about a sister.

To anyone else, the look was indiscernible but for a fraction of a second, Kristen saw what looked like utter distaste cross her husband's face before he masked it. He allowed the woman to pull him into a tight hug but immediately extricated himself.

"Hi, Jan."

"That's all the welcome I get? We haven't seen you in *years*."

"We saw you last Thanksgiving," he reminded her in the same flat tone.

"Yes, and then all that terrible business with your wife happened."

Kristen frowned and cleared her throat. The woman turned around and, as if noticing Kristen for the first time, exclaimed, "Oh! Hi, Kristen. Good to see you again."

Something was wrong. She knew she would have to ask Mark later but there was something off about the woman who stood in front of her. Kristen knew on an instinctive level that she would have to filter everything that came out of this woman's mouth to try and discern if it was sincere.

Mason cleared his throat and made the introduction. Mark continued to unload the car.

"Kristen, this is Jan, my wife."

Oh my God. Suddenly the pieces fell together. She looked at Jan again and knew she couldn't be more than five years Mark's senior. That was why he couldn't stand her. That was why he was cold towards his father. His dad had remarried less than a year after his mother's death and it was to a woman young enough to be his own daughter. Kristen tried to recover herself and smiled politely at Mark's stepmother.

"Nice to meet you."

Jan's superficial smile had disappeared at Kristen's look of shock. A nasty-nice smile replaced it as she remarked, "Oh, yeah. You can't remember *anything*. Well, we're glad to have you back. The kids were devastated when you left them."

Kristen frowned at the choice of words. So did Mark.

Jan continued, "It must be hard not recognizing your own family. I don't know what's worse - losing your mom in an accident or having one who doesn't remember you."

The words cut at Kristen and she tried her best to fortify her heart.

"Jan!" Mason chided his wife.

"What?" she exclaimed in imaginary innocence. "I'm just saying it must be difficult."

"It has been difficult," Mark said in a strained voice. "But we're making the best of it and are grateful to have her back. That's *obviously* better than not having her at all."

Kristen bypassed Jan and helped her husband wheel the luggage inside. Although, she really wanted to re-pack the car and take them all to a local hotel, she knew they were stuck until the weekend was over. She followed Mark up the wooden stairs to their log-lined guest room and watched as he settled their luggage next to the bed. His back to her, Kristen could make out the tense muscles lining his back and shoulders. She crossed the room and wrapped her arms around his torso, leaning her cheek against his shoulder blade. He stilled at her touch.

"I'm sorry," she whispered. "I didn't know."

He sighed deeply and calmly replied, "I know you didn't. It's not your fault."

She released his waist and sat down on the queen-sized bed, pulling his arm to take a seat next to her.

"Tell me," she said simply.

He sighed again. "There's not much to tell. My mom died on January 16th. In May, my dad told us that he met someone and by June, he was married to her. He didn't even wait six months."

"And she was…"

"Twenty-one. Fresh out of college. Young enough to be my sister. I turned eighteen in July and moved on campus early to get away from them. Emory was the only out of state school I had applied to. I never looked back."

"Has he ever acknowledged how-"

"How messed up it was - is?" He shook his head. "No. Just tries to pretend like we're one big happy family. Matt and Mike don't mind as much. They at least stayed in the same state. He sees them pretty often but we only visit once or twice a year."

"You should confront him," Kristen said.

He smiled. "You've been telling me to confront him since before we got married. I haven't done it yet and I won't do it until I know I won't lose it."

"Why can't you lose it?" she asked.

"I don't want to say something that will dishonor him and give him grief in his old age. Maybe I should have said something when he first did it but...I don't know..."

"Hindsight is always twenty-twenty."

He nodded in agreement.

"They never had kids?"

He shook his head. "That's one thing he put his foot down on. He got a vasectomy a year after they married. I was so mad at him I didn't even ask how the surgery went."

"He might have done it for you."

He gave her a dubious look. "Doubt it. It doesn't matter anyway. As far as I'm concerned, he spit on my mother's grave the minute he decided to marry her. I have to tolerate it but I don't have to like it."

She nodded, feeling as if a whole different side to him opened up right before her eyes. Kristen had imagined that Mark had a perfect family because he was such a kind and patient person. She now realized that much of his considerate nature probably stemmed from having such an inconsiderate father.

That night at dinner, she got to see the tension unfold right before her eyes as Mason tried on several occasions to engage his eldest in a conversation. Mark kept his responses short and to the point, refusing to make eye contact unless necessary.

Jan tried to tease her stepson, "Mark, you're so dull. Lighten up! Relax, won't you?"

Mark kept his cool and practically ignored her outright. The closest Kristen saw to him laughing was when he and his brothers mentioned their days as kids. Apparently Matt was the wild child of the group.

"How is it that you were supposed to look after me as the youngest but every time we were on base, I ended up chaperoning you?" Mike remarked. The men's laughter filled the large dining room.

Matt replied, "The only reason I let you tag along-"

"*Let* me?"

"Yeah, *let you*, was because Mark didn't have the patience for my mess. He'd either call Mom on me or drop me off at the nearest authority station. You just kept quiet and followed."

Mark rolled his eyes. "Half the time, you wanted Mom to straighten you out."

"Yeah, she had a way of disciplining you that made you feel loved all the same."

They quieted at the thought of her. Kristen cast a glance towards Mason and saw the look of a man slightly haunted. She knew in that moment that he still loved his late wife. Very much.

He looked at Mark. "Son-"

"Let's talk about something a little more cheerful, huh?" Jan shut the moment down and started chattering about the kids. Kristen noticed Mark's fist tighten around his fork. He kept his eyes on his plate and his thoughts to himself but as she glanced at his brothers, she could tell they too were offended by Jan's tactless interruption. Kristen reached under the table and rubbed her husband's leg. His fist loosened slightly and he glanced at her appreciatively. Jan continued, not seeming to notice any of the tension she had just created.

From what Kristen could observe, she seemed to care about the kids a great deal and even considered them her grandchildren. She did notice, however, that while Matt's and Mike's kids easily called Jan "Grandma," their kids specifically called her "Miss Jan."

"Savannah and Kylie picked a bushel of daisies by the creek down yonder and the twins showed Caleb how to saddle Jessup and Nora."

Kristen looked up from her plate. "By themselves? The boys saddled the horses by themselves?"

She glanced at Mark and noticed that he too held a frown of concern.

"Oh, they're big boys, Kristen, don't you worry."

Kristen shook her head and glanced at the second dining room where all the kids were congregated. "From now on, he needs to be with an adult before handling an animal of that size."

"Not a problem," Mason said. Matt and Tami agreed.

Jan scoffed, "You know, if you'd bring the babies down here more often, they'd be saddling and riding those mares by themselves easily."

"Maybe that's why we don't bring them down more often."

The men at the table chuckled at her quip. Mark leaned into her teasingly and she was glad to see him smile. But Jan's smile was long gone.

"We miss the children, Kristen." she said seriously. The room quieted.

"Jan," Tami began. "Maybe we should discuss this some other time-"

"I'm talking to my daughter-in-law, Tami." Jan said in a stern tone. Kristen raised her right brow in surprise. Who did this woman think she was? She looked at Jan's reddened face and took a deep breath.

"I'm sure you care about the kids a lot-"

"No, that's where you're wrong." she cut her off. "I don't just 'care' about those kids. I love 'em as if they were my own."

Mark frowned and said in a warning tone, "Jan."

"Maybe Mark won't tell you because he doesn't want to hurt your feelings but you weren't there when you left him alone with those kids."

"Are you serious?" Kristen snapped. "You say it like I left Mark for another man in Paris or something. I was in a serious accident. I could have been killed!"

"Well maybe that would have been better." Kristen, Tami, and Sienna all gasped. "At least these babies could have moved on and remembered you well. Now all they have is a woman who can't even remember giving birth to them."

BAM! The china rattled on the table as Mark's fist slammed down.

"That is enough!"

Kristen had never seen such a look of outrage pass his expression. His jaw was taut with fury and a vein ticked purple in his temple. He looked about ready to rip his father's wife apart, limb from limb. The room had gone completely quiet. The children's dining area had hushed as well. His brothers looked nervously between him and their stepmother, as though preparing to intervene if a fight broke out. Jan blanched and had long since shut up.

Matt tried to salvage things. "Mark-"

Mark put his hand up in warning. "Save it, Matt," he growled in a formidable tone.

He glared at Jan. "You say one more thing to or about my wife and so help me God, you will *never* see our children again."

She gasped. Mason sat forward.

"Mark," he said. "You don't really mean that-"

"Yes I do, Dad!" he replied, unyielding. "*Try* me."

He turned back to Jan who could do nothing but stare at Mark's face with wide eyes. Something told Kristen he had never snapped in front of the woman before.

"Do I make myself clear?" he asked her in an eerily calm tone. She nodded immediately.

Kristen placed a soothing hand on her husband's shoulder and felt some of the tension leave him instantly. The chair screeched across the floor as Mark pushed it back, stood up, left the room, and headed to the stairs. She watched her husband disappear up the stairs and turned back to see the entire table staring at her. She looked at her father-in-law and smiled weakly.

"I'm sorry."

"I've never seen him act like that," Jan huffed. The entire group ignored her.

"Is he going to be okay?" Tami asked

Mike nodded. "He'll always be okay. Mark has the heart of a lion. He can handle anything."

"Anything except someone messing with his wife," Matt remarked. They chuckled and Kristen couldn't help but join in.

"My son loves you very much," Mason remarked. He looked at her steadily. "Next to Jesus, you're the best thing that ever happened to him."

She didn't know what to say to that so she smiled and excused herself. She checked in on the kids who had long since picked up their conversation.

"Auntie Kris, is Uncle Mark okay?" Savannah asked, much in the same way Kylie would.

Kristen smiled and nodded. "Everything's fine. You guys having fun?"

The kids confirmed it exuberantly. She bid her own brood good night and joined her husband upstairs. By the time she walked in, he had already showered and changed. He was sitting up in their bed, reading a John Grisham novel.

"Hey," she said quietly. He looked up from his book and smiled a small smile.

"Hi."

"How you doing?" she asked.

He put the book down and rubbed the nape of his neck. "Okay, I guess." He lifted his eyes to hers. "I'm sorry I embarrassed you like that."

She frowned. "Embarrassed me? Are you kidding me? You rocked!"

"I did?"

"Absolutely! You stood up for me and defended me against your wicked stepmother."

He laughed, sobering when she joined him on the bed.

"My mom's birthday is tomorrow."

She looked at him in surprise. "She shared the same birthday as your dad?"

He nodded. "She would have been sixty-three if she had lived."

Kristen frowned. "No one mentioned it at the table."

"No one ever does," he quietly replied.

"I'm so sorry."

He smiled sadly at her and shrugged. "I've been toying with the idea to go out and see her grave. Lay some fresh flowers and maybe read some of her favorite psalms there."

"That's a wonderful idea. Can I go with you?" she asked.

He looked at her as though pleasantly surprised. "You'd really want to?"

"Of course."

He nodded. "Okay, let's do it."

He smiled and looked down at her mouth. She rolled her eyes, leaned in and enjoyed the feel of his soft lips moving over hers. She pulled back.

"I'm going to shower now."

She pulled her pajamas from her small suitcase and stepped into their adjoining bathroom. Even though it was a different bathroom in a different house, Kristen went about her routine as if she were back at home. She turned the shower on and let it run while she quickly brushed her teeth. She slid the shower door open and stepped in, expecting to feel the soothing sprays of nice hot water. To her dismay, she immediately felt the stinging spray of ice cold water directly on her back.

"Ahh!" she yelped. The door immediately swung open.

"Kristen, are you okay-?"

"Ahh!" she screamed again. There was no steam so he got a full view of her curvy, toned body. Mark quickly averted his eyes and she quickly pulled on her towel. She stepped out of the shower and he turned the water dial to warm.

"Why is it on cold?" she asked him incredulously.

"I'm sorry. I should have turned the dial back. I'm used to keeping it on cold," he said quietly, avoiding her eyes. He moved to leave the bathroom, but she caught a hold of his arm and pulled him back to face her. He finally met her eyes.

"Why?" she pressed.

"Because I take cold showers," he said in a calm voice.

She frowned. "Why on *earth* would you purposefully…?" She stopped mid-sentence as the realization washed over her, her eyes rounding into saucers. She watched as he closed his eyes and heat flushed his face.

"Oh! Oh, my God. Wow…" she stammered incoherently. Finally, she blurted out, "How long have you been doing this?"

He took a deep breath, looked around the bathroom and then finally landed on her eyes again. "Since you got back."

Her jaw dropped. "Every night?"

"And every day."

"Oh my God. Mark…"

He rolled his eyes. "Please don't look at me like that. Like I'm some kind of a freak-"

"No, I'm not!" she exclaimed. Quite the contrary. Her admiration for him grew all the more. He had been so patient and considerate with her and it was clearly costing him a great deal. She got sexually frustrated on a regular basis but she couldn't begin to imagine what it was like for him as a man.

He stepped around her and reached into the shower.

"The water's warm now," he said quietly. She nodded and watched as he stepped back out into their bedroom. And for a reason she couldn't quite put her finger on, she smiled.

"Happy birthday to you! Happy birthday to you! Happy birthday dear Grandpa! Happy birthday to you! Yay!"

The house erupted in cheers and applause as Mason Tyverson blew out the candles on his stack of buttermilk pancakes. Kristen loved that the family viewed a birthday as an all-day celebration. The kids were having a blast. They fed the chickens in the chicken coop, helped the farming staff harvest some of the crops, milked cows and rode horses. When they weren't doing a planned activity or farming chore, they mostly ran around the abundant land, playing hide-and-go-seek or tag. Kristen joined in a couple of times and she watched as her husband transitioned from a city-slick accountant to a rough-and-tumble rancher's son. He explained to her that shortly after his father retired from the Marines, his grandfather passed away and left the entire ranch to Mason Tyverson, his only son. The timing was perfect and Mason had been running the ranch for close to twenty years.

As his eldest son, Mark was entitled to the land but he had made it clear early on that he wanted nothing to do with it. So the property was held in trust, split equally amongst the three brothers, with Matt agreeing to handle the everyday running of it when their father did pass.

Still, it was interesting to see him ride horses, carry hay, and cut up wood. They were all activities that perfectly exhibited his tall, strong body. They hadn't discussed it but the previous night was the first time they had shared a room, much less a bed, since Kristen's return. Nothing had happened but in the middle of sleep, Mark had unconsciously pulled her into his arms. Kristen still remembered waking up to his strong embrace. She'd felt safe and warm and loved. She'd also felt an overwhelming desire for her husband.

Shortly after two in the afternoon, Kristen approached him as he chatted with Matt and Mike.

"You almost ready?" she asked. She didn't know if the others knew so she let nothing on.

Matt piped up, "Yeah, he's ready. We're going too if you don't mind."

She smiled widely at the three of them and gave her husband a kiss. "I'm glad he invited you."

"We are too," Mike said, punching his eldest brother in the arm.

The trip to the cemetery took less than twenty minutes and all three men arrived, carrying beautiful bouquets beside them. Tami and Sienna agreed to stay behind and watch the kids tasking Kristen with looking after the men, supporting them if they did indeed fall apart at their mother's grave. She held Mark's hand as they approached a simple, cement headstone which read:

"Michelle Lara Tyverson - Beloved Wife, Mother, and Woman of God - 1951 - 1992"

The three men took turns laying their bouquets at the foot of her headstone. They dusted off the dirt and cleared out the old flowers.

"Happy birthday, Mom." Mike whispered, his voice cracking just the slightest. Mark placed a steadying hand on his shoulder and rubbed it in comfort. He then pulled out his Bible and turned to Psalm 73. He read it aloud and followed it with Psalm 23. Finally, for their sakes, Kristen guessed, he read from Revelation, chapter twenty-one:

"'Then I saw a new heaven and a new earth. He will wipe every tear from their eyes. There will be no more death or mourning or crying or pain for the old order of things has passed away.'"

"Amen," a deep, southern voice agreed. All of them turned to find Mason standing behind them with tears in his tired brown eyes.

"Dad," Matt said nervously. "What are you doing here? I thought you went out with Jan."

"We got back early. Tami told me what y'all had planned and Sienna's keeping Jan occupied. I thought I'd pay your mother a visit since it's her birthday too."

Mike looked chagrined. "Dad, we didn't mean to leave you out or anything. We just wanted to…"

"I know, son. It's alright." He looked over at Mark. "This was your idea?"

Mark nodded.

"It was a good one. I miss her too."

Mark kept silent his eyes trained on the pickup truck his father had arrived in.

"I do miss her, Mark. You know that, don't you?"

"Of course we do, Dad." Matt replied.

"I'm talking to Mark. It's high time we talked this out. You're still mad at me. For what exactly, I don't know."

"You *don't know?*" Mark repeated, incredulously. "You don't know?"

"Is it Jan? Was it because of her age? How soon we got hitched?"

Mark looked around in astonishment. "I can't *believe* you right now. Mom suffered for ten months and the minute she died, you moved on to some *girl* who wasn't even five years older than me!"

"*Mark!*" Matt hissed but Mr. Tyverson held his hand up.

"No, let him get it out. It's been eating at him for all these years."

Mark shook his head at him. "I don't understand you. Mom adored you. She followed you wherever you decided to take us but the minute she was out of the picture, you moved on like nothing happened. Like she didn't even exist. Do you care? Did you ever?"

Kristen watched the exchange unfold. She was silent as the four men talked but was praying all the while.

Lord, please let this be the start of something new. Something good.

Mason took a deep breath and walked closer to his son. He saw the apprehension in his eldest's eyes and said in no uncertain terms. "I'm sorry, Mark."

Mark's jaw dropped. "What?"

"I'm sorry." He looked between him and the other men and continued in a humbled tone, "I care about Jan. She has her good points, she really does. But I...if I had to do it all over again, I would've done it differently."

They all knew what he meant but Kristen could appreciate him refusing to articulate it. It wasn't very loyal or kind to flat out say he should have never married his second wife.

He didn't hesitate to say, "It was wrong to re-commit so soon after your mother passed."

"Then why did you?" Mark asked.

"Because I hurt!" he cried out. The words sounded like they'd been ripped from his chest without the right anesthetic. "I hurt," he repeated in a quiet voice. "Your mother was the best thing that ever happened to me. She and I were supposed to be together for at least sixty years. She's supposed to be standing right next to me not laying down there." He gestured to her grave.

He looked at Mark meaningfully. "You know what it feels like." All four men glanced at Kristen. "Your heart came back to you from the dead. Mine didn't."

For the first time in twenty years, the veil of Mark's anger and resentment lifted just enough to see the situation through his father's eyes. He couldn't imagine doing what his father had done. He couldn't imagine replacing Kristen with a twenty-one-year-old just months after laying her to rest; but maybe he couldn't fathom it because that was precisely what his father had done. People grieved differently. He met his father's eyes again and could only think of one thing to say.

"I'm sorry, too. It hurts and I think you were wrong but I do love you. I'm sorry for not acting like it."

Kristen's eyes welled with tears as she watched Mason's fall freely down his ruddy cheeks. Her husband held his tears in check and she knew it was because he was in front of his younger brothers. Had he been looking, he would have seen the effect their exchange had, had on both men standing beside him. Mason extended his hand to Mark. But as Mark took it, he suddenly felt himself pulled into his father's strong arms and he gladly returned the hug. He pulled back slightly and looked at his brothers.

"Okay, pull it in, come on." All four men immediately mashed together as Kristen looked on. She grabbed her camera from her back pocket and captured the moment just seconds before they looked at her.

"Come on, Kris!"

"Yeah, get in here!"

"No kid left behind!"

She joined the group and felt warmth spread from the top of her head to the tips of her toes.

God was good.

"Unbelievable," an obnoxious female voice shattered the veil of peace. The group unfolded and turned to the source. Jan stood at the edge of the cemetery, her arms folded across her chest as she watched the scene with a sneer of irritation. Mason turned to his self-absorbed wife.

"Jan, don't start."

"Don't start?" she repeated. "Don't start? I have been slaving away for *months* trying to make this a nice birthday for you and you can't even show me the courtesy of trying to forget about the first one for just *one day*?"

Kristen couldn't believe her ears. Did she just refer to Mark's late mother as "the first one"?

"Jan," Matt remarked. "It's her birthday too. We were just celebrating her memory."

"What have I done to y'all? Really. What have I done? No matter what I do, no matter how much I love on your kids, I will never be considered a member of this family."

The men scoffed and shook their heads.

"Oh, come on."

"No, I'm serious!" she exclaimed. "Y'all are always talkin' 'bout her. Mase keeps her pictures up everywhere, Mark and Kristen's kids call *her*

'Grandma' and me 'Miss Jan' and every time y'all visit, Mark looks at me like I'm the devil!"

You might as well be, Kristen thought. She couldn't believe the woman had the gall to throw a hissy fit and ruin a perfectly beautiful moment like what they had just experienced. At the same time part of her felt almost sorry for Jan. She was clearly competing against the memory of a most-beloved woman – a competition she would never win. Kristen looked at her husband, surprised that he'd kept silent. Mark caught her eyes and smiled reassuringly.

He walked up to his father, hugged him once more and quietly said, "I'm glad I came, Dad. If only for that moment. Happy birthday. I love you. But Kristen and I are leaving tonight."

"What?" Matt exclaimed.

"Mark, don't go." Mike added.

He shook his head. "No, we need to. I don't want her," he said, referring to Jan, "to ruin everything we just achieved right now. Besides," he glanced at Kristen, "there are other things we need to attend to."

A chill raced down Kristen's spine at his words and the look in his eyes. She didn't know what he had in mind but she was eager to find out. The brothers continued to protest but Mason calmly nodded and gave his blessing for them to go. They drove back to the ranch, told the sisters-in-law and ordered the kids to hurry up and pack. Mark bumped their tickets up a day in advance and sprung for first class in order to guarantee the seats and also appease his very disappointed children.

By the time they arrived back in Atlanta, it was well after eight at night. Mark drove their family Hybrid out of town and into a suburb Kristen had only visited once. He pulled up to the end of the driveway and popped the locks.

"Aunt Dede!" Kylie exclaimed. The kids hopped out of the car and ran to the door just as Dierdra stepped out with her arms opened wide. She waved at the parked Hybrid and Mark waved back as he started the engine and backed out of the driveway again, fully aware of Kristen's questioning eyes.

They walked into the house and faced each other in the kitchen.

"You called Dierdra," she started.

"I did." He nodded.

"You wanted us to be alone. Why?"

Mark kept silent and watched her watch him.

"You said you had something to attend to back here. Did that have to do with me?"

He finally spoke. "I'm not blind, Kristen. I see the way you look at me and I know I'm not the only one who misses what we had."

"You mean sex?" she asked bluntly.

"I mean sex," he bluntly replied. He leaned against the kitchen island and looked down at his jean-clad lap. "I miss my wife. I miss *being* with you in the way we once were. If I learned anything from that trip home, seeing my dad *still* mourn over my mom…I just know I don't want to waste any more time if we don't have to. If I've read you wrong, then just tell me. I promise you, I won't push you if you're not ready. But I *know* you and I think you want what I want."

"I do."

He looked up at her, caught off guard by her frank admission. She didn't put up a token of resistance or a semblance of hesitation.

"Kiss me?" she asked softly. She didn't have to ask again. He closed the space between them immediately and covered her lips with his own. His kiss was soft, thorough and he didn't break it as he lifted her easily into his arms and carried her up the stairs to their bedroom. He lowered her to her feet, turned on the lights and once again, Kristen came face to face with their massive bed. She turned to him and silently began to disrobe. He did the same and in no time they stood across from each other, completely bare. They took in one another's bodies, as if seeing each other for the first time; and though nervous, Kristen was not ashamed. Instead, she felt an overwhelming, searing lust for him as she admired the sculpted planes of his athletic body. He was her husband and she had every right to make love to him. A right she would finally take advantage of.

"What is it?" he asked when she suddenly frowned.

"Protection…?"

He shook his head. "You had a tubal ligation after Kylie."

She nodded, her heart pounding. He took a step forward.

"Are you sure you want to do this?" he asked her, almost warningly. "Kristen, once we start, I will not be able to stop. You cannot change your mind on me."

His tone was firm and unwavering, not the gentle, patient tone she was used to hearing from him. He wanted her then and there but he pushed every ounce of his being to wait and get a clear answer from her. Months of pent up sexual frustration, months of daily cold showers…his body was beyond ready and he knew himself enough to know he could not turn back if she changed her mind.

Kristen looked into Mark's cognac eyes, her body trembling but from what, she didn't know. Her heart thundered in the cavity of her chest and her senses stood on end. Despite her frenetic physical state, her decision was rock solid.

She nodded. "I'm sure."

The words barely left her mouth before Mark was in motion. He crossed the room quickly and deftly took her mouth with his own. He lifted her onto the bed and laid his solid frame across hers. She shivered at the contact of their skin. She could feel him tremble and knew it was due to his extended celibacy. Despite her "inexperience," despite her having no recollection of making love with him or any other, Kristen knew what was going on…for the most part at least. His hands were everywhere. His mouth buried firmly in the curve of her neck, Kristen gasped loudly as Mark's fingertips danced and teased over the erogenous zones of her body.

He knows my spots, she surmised as she saw him smile in reaction to her gasp. *What else does he know? What does he know that I don't?*

Mark felt her fingers tense at his shoulders and reminded himself that it was all new for her, at least psychologically. It was as if it was her first time, just like it had been ten years ago. He pulled away just slightly to meet her eyes. Though clouded with desire, Kristen could see the tenderness in them.

"You're okay," he said reassuringly, his voice hoarse. "You're okay."

It was all she needed to hear. Her body immediately relaxed and he bent to her lips again. He cloaked her body with his own and the two became one. Kristen, swept away in the sensation of it all, began to close her eyes.

"Keep them open," Mark commanded huskily. "Look at me."

An indescribable joy filled her heart as she met her husband's eyes. She looked up at him as he watched her with open adoration and desire.

"I've missed you so much," he gasped.

He loved her intentionally, selflessly; and though he found immense pleasure in their union, it was amplified by witnessing her wonder at their lovemaking. He watched her closely, teased her relentlessly, and pleased her thoroughly. Kristen smiled as she realized she was one with her husband. Doing a marriage ritual Adam and Eve had done so long ago. A feeling of unadulterated pleasure gripped her like bands of steel. She felt both out of body and completely anchored as they moved together, relearning each other's rhythm. They gave, they took, and they peaked to heights neither thought they could reach.

Foreheads touching, they gasped against one another, fighting to catch their breaths. His eyes closed, Mark silently prayed.

Thank you, Lord. Thank you.

He raised his head again and met her eyes. She looked up at him and could see tears glistening in his. His look was so tender she didn't know how to respond. He smiled as a couple drops escaped.

"I love you," he said simply.

As she looked into his eyes, she knew she was looking at the very depths of his soul. There was no deception. No ulterior motive. Just love. Did her eyes reflect the same?

"You don't have to say it," he whispered. "I understand."

And with that, he reclaimed her lips and planted a tender kiss on them. He rolled to his side of the bed and drew her tightly against him with both arms. He could feel her shivering and drew her tighter, stroking the length of her arms with his thumbs. They both remained silent for long moments, both deep in thought. Mark watched her as she lay completely still, as if in shock.

He finally asked, "Are you okay?"

She nodded. He fished some more.

"Did I hurt you?"

She looked up at him in surprise.

"No. Why would you think that?"

He shrugged, a blush rising to his cheeks. "Just making sure."

"I'm okay, Mark." She smiled. "I'm *better* than okay, actually."

She looked down at her hand on his chest, the nervous bride again.

"Is it...is it *always* like this?" she asked.

"Like what?"

"Earth shattering?" she blurted out.

Mark chuckled warmly, glad that she'd found as much pleasure in their lovemaking as he did.

He nodded, his expression sobering. "Yes."

She bit her bottom lip and looked up at him. His eyes were inviting and satisfied.

"Then I want to do it again."

They made love well into the night and finally surrendered their bodies to the inevitable exhaustion. The next morning, she awoke in his arms and looked up at his chiseled jaw. The man looked like he was cut out of stone. Mark began to stir and she moved slightly to accommodate him. As soon as she moved, she felt the soreness. She was sore from head to toe, mostly between her legs. Muscles she didn't even know existed ached.

It was a good ache.

He roused fully from his sleep and his eyes immediately landed on her in his arms. He smiled warmly and instinctively tightened his grip on her. She smiled back as he pulled her up to him, sore muscles and all, and kissed her deeply.

He rubbed her back in intimate circles and asked her tenderly, "Breakfast?"

She nodded.

"Great. I'll cook. You shower."

He kissed her again then stood to retrieve his boxers. She looked at him admiringly and he grinned as she brazenly watched him dress. When he left the room, she got up and took her shower. The warm water helped with her sore muscles. But when she stepped out, the mental onslaught began. She dried herself and stood in front of the foggy mirror. All she could see were the stretch marks, cellulite, and flesh that weren't tight and toned. She'd been able to ignore it when she was with him the night before but as she looked at herself in the daylight, all of her anxiety rushed back at her. She ignored the muscles and taut areas of her body and picked at the itty-bitty fat on her flat stomach.

I should have gone to the gym this morning. She pinched harder. *What does he see in me?*

So fixed was she on the image in front of her, the flesh between her fingers, that she gasped at the feel of two strong arms slipping around her waist. He insistently moved her hands away from her belly and covered it with his own. He squeezed her to him and whispered one simple word.

"Flawless."

Kristen tried to pull out of his arms but he held her tightly to his chest.

"I don't care how long it takes, Kristen, but I'm going to get that crazy notion out of your head that you are anything less than perfect to me."

"Whatever, Mark."

He whipped her around, grasped the back of her neck and pulled her mouth to his. His kiss was demanding, dominant, but his hands were gentle and tender as he moved her against the wall and hitched her up to meet his hips. Their joining was quick, frenzied, and utterly satisfying. Kristen laid her head onto Mark's heaving shoulders; he held them both in spite of his exhaustion and leaned the majority of his weight on the wall behind Kristen, balancing with one arm and holding her with the other.

Slightly recovered, Kristen turned to Mark and whispered, "Look at what you've done. Now I have to shower all over again."

He grinned shamelessly and replied, "Good. I'll join you."

CHAPTER ELEVEN
Go Home

"Caleb's grades haven't improved." Kristen remarked. The kids were back in school and trying to finish the semester strong but Caleb's scores were still lackluster at best. Even with all the healing and bonding that had taken place between Caleb and Kristen, his school work was a sore spot in his life. Kristen could see how each grade bruised her son's self-esteem and it worried her.

Mark sighed. He too saw the red marked scores and he was very aware of the fact that they were running out of time to turn things around. The tutor seemed to be doing his job. From what he could see, Caleb's writing had improved – but it didn't seem to impress his teacher. Mark cooked dinner while Kristen prepared their afternoon snacks. The kids would be back very soon.

"You know the end of the year third-grader awards are this evening," she said. He nodded.

"Were you planning on going?"

He nodded. "I wanted to talk to Principal Lane and a couple board members. But I just accepted a new client. He's in the middle of an audit and needs an expert."

She nodded. "Then I'll go."

"Are you sure?"

"Yeah. I have yet to meet the principal and I want to see if Caleb wins anything."

The ceremony was dry and dull and unfortunately Caleb didn't win anything. A Joshua Callahan was the star of the night. A short blonde boy with bright blue eyes, he was called to the stage on numerous occasions to accept whatever award Ms. Walker had written in his honor. Kristen looked at the front of the small auditorium and noticed his parents loudly applaud him every time his name was called. Dressed in swanky cocktail attire, Mr. and Mrs. Callahan stood out from the crowd and were a stone's throw away from several of the guests whose pins indicated them as board members.

They're connected and rich, Kristen observed.

As if reading her mind, a woman behind her remarked to her friend. "No classmate of his stands a chance when that little boy is around. His parents will buy him the valedictorian seat at Harvard if they get the chance."

When the awards were over, they stepped out onto the school patio for refreshments. She looked down at her son beside her. Dressed in a small suit and shiny dress shoes, Kristen complimented him on how dapper he looked.

He smiled and replied, "Mom, no one says 'dapper' anymore."

She smiled back. "Well, I'm glad you know what it means. Most kids your age don't even know that."

They milled around the room as Kristen made several new acquaintances. A Shannon Shirer introduced herself:

"Kristen, so good to see you. We were on the same PTSO committee last year. Hi, Caleb!" Her son waved at the woman affectionately. "How are you doing this year? Have you liked your classes since the transfer?"

He quietly shook his head and Kristen's heart ached for him.

"He hasn't had the best time in Ms. Walker's class. His writing is a little behind."

Shannon frowned in surprise. "Really? He was doing so well in Ms. Carver's class. He was the top student there, *especially* in writing."

Kristen frowned. "Really?"

"Absolutely! A+ average, he was the 'valedictorian' of the class that semester. Ms. Carver said the quality of his writing was eons ahead of his classmates. I was certain it would be this semester too."

Heat suffused Kristen's senses as she excused herself from Shannon's presence.

"Caleb, why don't you go play on the playground a bit? I'll be right back."

It all clicked in her mind. His low scores. The Callahan kid's success. Could it be that she and Mark were wrong the whole time? That Caleb really had been doing his best, despite the circumstances at home?

No classmate of his stands a chance when that little boy is around. His parents will buy him the valedictorian seat at Harvard if they get the chance.

Ms. Walker was standing near the punch stand, the principal, a tall Asian man in his forties, to her left and Mr. Callahan to her right.

"Mrs. Tyverson!" she said brightly. "Lovely to see you."

Kristen almost wanted to applaud her for her insincere welcome. She should have gone into acting instead of teaching. The tall imposing man to Ms. Walker's right extended his hand.

"Mitch Callahan," he said with a slight smirk. "We've met before but I heard you might not remember."

Jerk.

She shook his hand and gave him an icy smile.

"Ms. Walker, Principal Lane, may I speak with you alone for a moment?" Her tone was unyielding and their expressions quickly shifted to those of wariness.

"Of course," Ms. Walker said in a strained voice. Mr. Callahan excused himself and wandered to a nearby group.

"As you already know, Ms. Walker, I am very concerned about my son's progress at this academy."

"Mrs. Tyverson," Principal Lane interrupted. "Could we not discuss this matter at a later time? We try not to bring these issues up during celebratory functions."

"I understand that Principal Lane, which is why I was merely asking if we could set up a time to meet."

"You can contact the front office to arrange a time." Ms. Walker said.

"That's just it," Kristen countered. "I have called the front office before and the receptionist, Ms. Bentley, has informed me that all parent-teacher conferences are arranged directly with the teacher. I have emailed you and never receive an answer to my questions but merely a direction to set up a time with the receptionist. I'm getting the run-around here."

Ms. Walker frowned and glanced at Principal Lane nervously. He frowned as well.

"Mrs. Tyverson, I'm terribly sorry for the miscommunication that has taken place. There have been several policy changes and sometimes the receptionist can lose track of what the current policy is."

Kristen shook her head, sick of the unnecessary information.

"Look, all I want is to discuss why my son's writing is not meeting your criteria and what he can do to improve it. He's running out of time this semester and I'm frustrated because this should have been addressed months ago."

The teacher looked taken aback by Kristen's direct, no-nonsense approach.

"I - I beg your pardon?"

"You heard me. His grades are suffering and his morale is low because there hasn't been a change for months and there hasn't been a change for months because every time I've contacted you or the staff at this school, I can't be given the time for a single meeting or a straight answer." Her voice was beginning to rise in her frustration. Out of her peripheral vision, she could see several groups stopping to look at them.

"Mrs. Tyverson, I give your son the grade he deserves."

"I beg to differ, Ms. Walker. I recognize that I bear some bias as his parent, but his writing is well above the average student in his grade and his father and I check his assignments on a regular basis. Unless you can provide an example of what his work should look like, we are at a loss for what to do."

"Is this really the place to discuss such issues?" Mr. Callahan stepped in. His towering 6'2" frame was no match for Mark's height and stature but her husband wasn't there and Kristen suddenly felt uneasy in his presence. She didn't let it show, though.

Her back straight and eyes direct, she stood up to the overbearing man and said, "Excuse me, but this doesn't concern you."

He spoke as if she hadn't said anything. "I can assure you Ms. Walker is a fair teacher. Challenging, but fair. I appreciate an instructor who doesn't coddle children. My son is in the same class and is flourishing."

"Good for him," Kristen said. She turned to Ms. Walker and blocked Callahan out. "All I want is to help Caleb improve."

"Hire a tutor," Callahan bit out.

"We already have." She refused to meet his eyes and watched as Ms. Walker squirmed under her scrutiny. "If we know what your expectations are for his writing, I know he can get there. Shannon Shirer was just telling me how well he did in Ms. Carver's class last semester. He was at the top of his class."

Callahan's handsome face crimpled into a nasty frown and he came within inches of her frame.

"Kristen, Joshua is at the top of his class because he *earned* it! Your son would be if he did the same. I don't know how hard you must have hit your head in Afghanistan—"

Kristen gasped.

"—but maybe you should focus on getting it back on straight before worrying about your son's place in class and harassing teachers like Ms. Walker. It doesn't suit you."

Kristen saw red. She could feel an oppressing heat crowd around her collar and all she wanted to do was blow steam.

"Mrs. Tyverson, Mr. Callahan-"

"This is none of your business. It's a private conversation that concerns my child and unless I bring yours up, why don't you do us all a favor and go back to the gold-encrusted corner you came from?"

Callahan closed the small space threateningly. "How dare you-"

"Get away from her!" Suddenly, two small hands shoved at the man's pants and pushed him away with all his might. Unprepared for the nine-year-old's interference, Mitch Callahan immediately fell backwards and toppled over onto the punch-bowled table, red juice spilling everywhere...

"I told you I was handling it," Mark said in clear agitation.

"Handling it *how*? Mark, school ends in less than a month!" Kristen countered.

She looked at Mark across the kitchen island and could almost feel his frustration bristling against her skin. She'd never seen him so upset before. Well, she had, but never at *her*. Gone was the patient, long suffering husband, and in his place, a really pissed off father. The kids looked on in rapt attention as both adults spoke to each other, seemingly unaware of anyone else in the room.

"It doesn't matter now," Mark said snidely. "Now, Caleb is suspended and we have to figure out how this will affect his education and his future! He's lucky he didn't get thrown out!"

"I didn't mean for him to get in trouble, Mark. He was just defending me. You should have seen how that Callahan jerk was getting in my face." Kristen said.

She still couldn't understand how their son could get penalized for simply standing up for her. Mark felt a small sense of guilt for not having been there to defend Kristen himself. Regardless of what she had said, he wouldn't have allowed any man to get in close proximity to her, especially in a threatening manner. Part of him was proud of his son for standing up for her; but it was currently buried in the midst of a really stressful situation.

"I should've taken him instead." Mark shook his head. "In fact, I should have just gone *alone*."

Kristen winced. As disastrous as things had turned out, it hurt her that he openly regretted allowing her to take Caleb to the function. Her confidence as the mother in their family was slowly beginning to erode the more he spoke and she just wanted him to stop. Jasmine looked at her mother's face and could almost see the thoughts displayed like text on a jumbotron. Normally, her dad would have noticed but with one glance at his face, she knew he was too upset to observe it. She tried to intervene before it got worse.

"Dad, Mom was just trying to help. I'm the one who told her about his grades in the first place."

"No," Kylie piped up. "I did."

Mark shook his head in frustration.

"Like I said, it doesn't matter now." He gestured to their son. "Caleb is suspended and he has a mark on his permanent record."

Kristen felt the dig and it bristled.

"Come on, does it really matter?" Kristen asked in irritation. Mark looked at her incredulously.

"Does it matter?" he repeated.

"Yes," she said, struggling to stay calm. "He's in third grade. This should hardly prevent him from going to college or living a productive life."

"Kristen, he'll never be considered by a decent private school *until* college! And then, he won't be able to get in. This is how delinquents start. A suspension here, an expulsion there."

"Dad!" Jasmine admonished. She glanced at Caleb, who was frowning. Mark looked from his daughters to his son and knew he had crossed the line.

"I'm sorry, Caleb. I know you're a good kid. I just don't want this to become a pattern."

Caleb shrugged his shoulders and kept silent.

He's being ridiculous, Kristen thought. And on some subconscious level, Mark knew it as well. But in the heat of the moment, Mark wanted nothing more than to make her realize how much she'd blown it; how much she should have just trusted him and allowed him to take the lead in this particular situation. He'd had a plan and now it wouldn't work because of the suspension. It was also driving him crazy that she was carrying such a nonchalant attitude about it. Mark could hear a still voice urging him to calm down:

Love is patient. Love is kind...

Does she even care? he thought.

It is not easily angered.

Is she even thinking about this as a mother?

Kristen knew she had messed up. She felt terrible about Caleb's suspension and angry about the circumstances surrounding it. What she couldn't understand was Mark's incessant harping about it. He was suspended - the decision had been made; she was ready to move on and come up with a plan of attack. How would she expose that witch of a teacher for what she really was? And how could she convince the principal to see Caleb for his true character, not what that idiot Callahan tried to portray?

She sighed, picked up her purse and turned to go upstairs.

"I'll talk to Principal Lane tomorrow," she said over her shoulder.

"No, you won't." The response was swift, decisive, and delivered in a condescending tone.

Kristen turned to face her husband and saw a look of determination in his eyes. For the first time, she looked at him and really didn't like what she saw.

"I'll figure this out, Mark." She glanced at their son. "I got Caleb into this and I'll get him out."

But Mark was shaking his head before she even finished her sentence.

Mark... He ignored the voice.

"No. Leave it alone. *I'll* figure this out."

"I want to make this right."

"Like you tried to make it right before?" he snapped. "No. Leave it alone and let me handle it, before you make an even bigger mess of things."

The words felt like a slap across the face to her. She was really about to boil.

"Dad, maybe she can help-"

"Enough, Jasmine!" Mark snapped. His daughter frowned in surprise.

Kristen finally lost her cool.

"What is wrong with you?"

The kids looked at each other in apprehension. Once again, their parents were tuning them out.

"Nothing is wrong with me," he said in a strained tone. "I'm just a father looking out for his kid."

Love is patient. Love is kind.

He didn't want to hear it. She was pushing his buttons and in conjunction with his exhaustion, he was about to boil over too.

"And I'm a mother looking out for mine."

"Just leave this alone, Kristen."

"Why are you so hell bent on shutting me out? He's my son too, in case you've forgotten."

He snapped.

"In case *I've* forgotten? You're the only one doing the forgetting!"

Kristen gasped. Jasmine looked at her father.

"Dad-"

Mark ignored her.

"Oh, so *now* you suddenly remember? You haven't been in the game for *months* and *now* you're so eager to get involved?"

Silence.

Kristen stared at Mark, her mouth ajar. She couldn't believe he'd just thrown that in her face. Not only did his words hurt her to her core, she was suddenly acutely aware of the kids' presence in the room. A feeling of embarrassment washed over her. She glanced at them and saw that they all had varying expressions of horror. Kylie held tears in her eyes that Kristen was beginning to mirror.

Mark regretted the words as soon as he uttered them. Like Kristen, he too looked over at his children. His anger dissolved and he was filled with an unspeakable shame at having allowed them to witness such a fight. He didn't know what horrified him more; his children's hurt expressions or the look of betrayal in his wife's tear-filled eyes. He locked eyes with her and tried to communicate all of his regret in one look.

"Kristen-"

She didn't give him the satisfaction. She went to the kids and softly whispered:

"Sorry, guys. Get some sleep. I love you."

"What's going to happen now?" Jasmine asked, not sure exactly what she was asking.

"Your dad will figure it out."

"Kristen…"

She felt his eyes on her but ignored him as she gave them each a brief hug and turned on her heel without a backward glance.

"Kristen, I'm sorry."

She quickly walked up the stairs and into their bedroom. Her heart shut down and tried to barricade itself from the tide of hurt, betrayal, anger, and confusion that threatened to overwhelm it. Her mind went into tunnel mode. She pulled out a small duffel bag and quickly stuffed it with clothes. She changed into a pair of jeans and a casual shirt and tried to ignore the sound of Mark apologizing to the kids downstairs. As they migrated upstairs and began to get ready for bed in their separate rooms, Kristen finished the last of her packing and made her way to the stairs.

Mark saw her just as he was leaving Kylie's room.

"Kristen, I'm so sorr-" He saw her bag. "Where are you going?"

"Out."

"Out where?"

She didn't respond but continued to jet down the stairs and into the kitchen, on her way to the garage. She heard him following behind and quickly picked up her pace.

So did he.

"Don't do this. Please! I'm sorry. I didn't mean what I said-"

She swung the garage door open, turned the lock and quickly shut it behind her. Her keys in hand, she pressed the button to open the garage, popped open the locks of her car and climbed in, all without stopping.

Mark was half-running at that point.

Please don't let her leave, Lord. Not like this.

He fumbled with the garage door before realizing she had locked it. By the time he opened it, she was backing her car out of the garage and down the driveway—

"Kristen!"

—driving into the night with no hint as to where she was going.

Her heart was pounding. Kristen felt her joints loosen and her muscles fire up as she slammed her feet onto the treadmill as it whirred. She zoned out and focused on the music in her ipod. But her mind wasn't on the music. And it wasn't on the run. It kept flashing to their home; over and over…the words replaying like a broken record in her memory.

"You haven't been in the game for months *and* now *you're eager to get involved?"*

She didn't know how to process it. It was their first fight. Or at least the first fight they'd had since she returned. Married couples fought – she knew that. And she should have known it was just a matter of time before they did. But it had caught her off guard. She had allowed herself to be lulled into the comfort of their relationship, their family, his love.

No one's perfect, Kristen.

I know that. Of course he has his faults but that argument came out of nowhere. And even when a fight was to come, I never thought he would be so nasty about it.

When Jan had brought up her memory loss or Callahan had used it to insult her, Kristen was insulted but not particularly surprised. Neither people had allegiance to her or any motivation to be sensitive of her feelings. But the one person who had always been patient, considerate and quick to defend her suddenly used her condition against her. And in front of their kids. He'd not only hurt her feelings but embarrassed her and undermined her authority in front of the very children he had encouraged her to step up and mother again. The whole thing confused her. And in her confusion and hurt, anger quickly took root.

Her feet still moved and her arms were in sync. A steady rhythm began to tease her mind and drive her crazy. With each step on the treadmill, each swoosh of the machine, Kristen could hear: *"What now? What now? What now?"*

Images flashed in her mind of the ceremony, the fight with Callahan, the red punch spilling all over his head and suit. The fight in the kitchen. Mark's angry brown eyes. The tears in Kylie's eyes. Jasmine's attempts to mediate. Caleb's frown of confusion.

Suddenly, Kristen felt herself stumble. She fell out of sync with the machine and her heart pounded in fear as she tried to catch herself. She couldn't. She fell forward and instinctively placed her arm on the running treadmill. A searing burn shot up her right forearm as her body tumbled down the tread and off the machine. Within seconds, she was surrounded by staff and fellow gym attendants.

"Miss, are you alright?"

"What happened?"

"Somebody get us a towel! She's bleeding."

He was right. Her forearm had gotten caught in the lining of the running treadmill and had sliced the skin open. The staff members shooed the other attendants away and helped her stand. They escorted Kristen to a private office and gave her water to cool off. When the worst of the bleeding stopped, she begged them off and went to her locker. As she pulled out her bag, her cell phone buzzed.

She'd missed twenty-eight calls. The incoming one wasn't from Mark but Dierdra.

"Hello?" she said.

"Will you please come over? What's the point of having girlfriends if you're not going to dish about the latest fight?"

"You need to go home," Dierdra finally said after Kristen finished her story. They'd been sitting in Dierdra's immaculate living room for well over an hour. Horrified to see her best friend bleeding and drenched in sweat,

Dierdra immediately treated Kristen's arm. Ensuring that it didn't need stitches, she flushed out the wound with antibiotics and Neosporin, gave her some Advil for the pain, and allowed her to use her guest room shower.

"Go home?" Kristen asked. "Didn't you hear a single thing I said?"

"I heard everything you said and I still say you need to go home. Krissy, you're running away from your problems, not facing them head on and as a grown woman with three kids, you owe it to yourself and your family to work things out with your husband. This too shall pass."

She's on his side. As far as she's concerned he did nothing wrong.

Kristen...

It was just her name. But as soon as she heard that gentle voice of rebuke, Kristen checked herself. It wasn't about sides. It was about her family and the need to move forward.

"I don't know if I can do this, Dee."

"What do you mean?" she asked. Her eyes held no judgment and unlike the last time they'd talked, she simply listened and waited to hear Kristen's heart.

"I don't remember signing up for this. I don't remember the pre-marital counseling and what to do when you fight. Dede, his reaction came out of *nowhere* – I've never seen him so mad over something so small."

Dierdra frowned. "Could it be a cultural thing? Maybe grades and academics are much more important to him than you thought."

"If that was the case, he would have stormed into the school months ago at the first sign of Caleb's grades dropping."

Dierdra nodded. "Okay... Is he stressed? Could it be a buildup of things? Kristen, he's been through a lot, too."

"But why now?"

"Well, put yourself in his shoes. Imagine: he's just gotten closer to you and then – *bam* – this happens. Maybe he just misdirected his frustration."

Well, he certainly expressed it clearly.

Kristen...

There it was again. That voice. She took a deep breath and tried to process what Dierdra just told her. Maybe it was just misdirected frustration. He was wrong but so was she in the way she had tried to handle Caleb's situation without her husband's input. They both were wrong for arguing in front of their children. And she probably hadn't helped matters by leaving the house without any clue as to where she was going. When she'd left, her phone had buzzed nonstop. She'd missed more than forty calls. It suddenly occurred to her that Mark had stopped calling more than an hour ago, shortly after she'd arrived at Dierdra's.

"You told him I was here, didn't you?"

Dierdra nodded. Kristen remembered her words when she called at the gym.

"He told you about the fight before you called, didn't he?"

"He wanted to know if you were with me and you weren't so I called you. He was really scared, Kristen."

Kristen sighed. She didn't know what to make of all of it.

"You need to go home," Dierdra repeated. "Marriage is hard – even with the best of men. But the ones that last are the ones where *both* parties stay. You need to go home."

She turned the lock in the door and quietly entered the house. He was waiting in the kitchen and straightened as she entered. The relief on Mark's face was palpable. His eyes were red and bleary. He looked like he had just weathered a storm but kept his words simple.

"Hi."

She nodded at him and moved to go to the stairs when she felt his hand touch her arm. He frowned at the bandage.

"What happened?" he asked, concern written all over his face.

She kept her tone flat, her eyes averted. "I fell on the treadmill. It's fine."

"Kristen, I-"

"Mark, I'm tired. My arm hurts and so does my head. I can't talk about this right now."

She finally met his eyes and saw the hurt. But in that moment, she didn't care. She felt numb and raw at the same time and wanted to distance herself from him. He could read it all on her face and he slowly nodded.

"Tomorrow, then." he whispered. She nodded and went to the stairs. He followed slowly and kept his distance but spoke when she reached the top of the stairs and turned towards the guest room.

"Not there," he said quietly. She stopped and turned to face him, challenge lit in her eyes.

He almost backed down but held his resolve.

"We're married. We're going to fight. We've fought before. But as long as you and I are husband and wife, we will share the same bed."

She frowned. Hadn't they slept in separate beds only weeks ago?

It was as if he'd read her mind because he then said, "That was different. You didn't know me and I didn't want to force myself on you. But you *know* me now." She felt heat rise to her face at the meaning behind his words. "And I *know* you. You want to wait 'till tomorrow to talk it out, that's fine, but as long as we're married, we will sleep in the same bed, angry or not."

He watched her grapple with his challenge, the value behind his words, and the biblical call for her to submit to him and his request. He saw the anger, hurt, and insecurity flash right before his eyes and he wished they could talk it out then and there. But he also knew not to push her for more – she was already at her limit and was literally in pain. He glanced at her arm, curious about how she fell. Was it a simple accident? Or was she so distracted by their fight that she completely lost concentration and injured herself as a result?

He felt a deepening remorse at the thought and it showed in his eyes. She saw it and felt her anger mitigate, if only slightly. She wordlessly turned and walked into their room. She quickly changed, climbed into bed and tried to fall asleep. For some reason, it didn't happen until she felt his weight sink in the bed beside her. He didn't touch her. He didn't hold her. But she felt his presence all the same and sleep finally came.

CHAPTER TWELVE
The Next Day

Kristen woke up with a throbbing pain radiating from her right arm. She took a deep breath and sat up in bed. The events from the previous night rushed to her memory uninvited and a sense of hurt mingled with anger filled her chest.

She stood on shaky legs and realized that she was still in their bedroom. It was light out but Mark had drawn the curtains to allow her more time to rest. She looked over at her nightstand and saw a glass of water standing next to a small saucer with two Advils waiting for her. His consideration annoyed her. He was making it hard for her to stay angry. On one hand, it was just like him to do something so thoughtful. On the other hand, she didn't know which man to expect after the fight they'd had. She didn't want to open herself up to him again.

She looked at the clock. She had just under an hour to get ready and head to work. She knew it wasn't going to happen so she called the producer and had the shoot pushed back a couple of hours. She brushed her teeth, rinsed her face, changed the bandage on her arm and made her way down to the kitchen.

He stood at the island with a kind look in his eyes.

"Hi," he said softly. "How's your arm?"

She frowned. He didn't seem mad at her and while she was grateful for the grace he extended her, she couldn't help but remember all of the things he'd said before.

Don't fall for the nice guy act.

She silently walked to the fridge and poured herself some orange juice and felt the stiffness in her right arm. Hopefully the Advil would kick in soon.

He left it for you, a small voice reminded her.

Mark watched her ignore him and sighed. He could almost feel the wall she built around her and he knew he'd given her the tools to build it.

He tried again. "We should change your bandage."

"I already did," she replied before sipping her juice.

She kept her eyes on the cup as she drank. When she finished, she put it in the sink and filled it with water.

"Kristen, look at me."

She turned from the sink and met his eyes, her own giving nothing away.

"I'm sorry. I'm so sorry for what I said to you last night. I lost my temper and I hurt you in my own anger."

"Why were you so angry?" she asked.

He nodded, expecting the question. "There's no excuse, really. I overreacted. You and I were just getting back on track and then this happened. I wasn't angry so much at you or Caleb or the situation. I think I was just angry at the constant onslaught of things going wrong. If it wasn't one thing, it was another. I should have been yelling out to God but instead I yelled at you."

He waited for her to respond but she didn't. She just looked at him with the same empty expression.

"I don't want to lose you," he said suddenly. He could feel tears coming to his eyes but he looked down and held them in check. He wasn't afraid to cry but he was tired of the constant water works. He couldn't believe one woman could pull so many tears out of him in such a short span of time.

Kristen could feel her own tears welling. Their relationship, just getting on track, was re-fractured and she couldn't find it in her heart to plaster the cracks.

"You hurt me," she said softly. He looked back up, surprised that she had spoken.

"I know I did."

"I feel like I don't know who you are anymore. You've been so patient and kind and steady and then this…"

He looked down at his hands then back up at her eyes.

He shrugged. "I'm human. I'm not a perfect man but I try to be the best I can in Christ. But still, I screw up. I really am sorry, Kristen."

He didn't know what else to say. If he did, he would have said it, if only to get the distant look off her face. *How can I get her back? I just gained her trust. How did I lose it so soon?*

Kristen spoke up, "I was wrong for running off the way I did. I'm sorry. It was childish and immature. I - I…" She struggled for words.

He nodded. "I understand why you did it."

She opened her mouth but closed it again.

When she opened it once more, it was to ask, "Where's Caleb?"

He couldn't hide the disappointment at the change of subject.

"He's with Janet. I wanted us to talk alone."

She nodded.

"What do we - what happens now?" she asked.

"You mean what do we do?"

She shook her head and raised her hands. "You made it clear that you call the shots where the kids are concerned. I shouldn't have intervened."

"No!" he cried. "No, I was *wrong. Kristen.* I was angry and stupid and I railroaded over you in front of our children. I will *never* do that to you again. I want you to be the mom and my partner in raising our kids. I'm sorry."

She kept silent, mulling his words over in her mind. He knew they hadn't sunken into her heart yet. He retrieved a manila folder from the family computer desk and handed it to his wife. She took it from him, careful not to touch his fingers. She flipped it open and saw two sets of all of Caleb's assignments - the work he had done and the work of another student: Joshua Callahan!

"How did you get these?" she asked in astonishment.

"Caleb and Josh are friends."

Her head snapped up in surprise. She had no idea.

"Josh has been giving Caleb several of his graded writing assignments, hoping to help Caleb improve. The problem is, Caleb's writing is actually better than Josh's."

Kristen nodded. She could already see several syntax and grammatical errors in the other boy's writing and yet he had the higher grade.

Mark continued, "I've been photocopying them, building a file. The ultimate goal was to help Caleb."

Kristen nodded.

"I was planning on presenting enough assignments like this to the board and principal in order to get them re-graded and reassessed. All this time, I thought his grades were just a result of his issues. But after seeing these assignments and hearing what you observed yesterday, I'm beginning to wonder what role Ms. Walker really plays in all this." He shrugged again. "But whether or not she has an arrangement with Josh's parents is beside the point. Writing is a subjective thing to grade. We would need a smoking gun to prove all of that."

"Which would be...?"

"Some sort of acknowledgment on Ms. Walker's part of deliberately lowering Caleb's grades. Unless we have definitive proof, it's 'he said, she said.' The grades aren't enough to prove she's scheming with them."

"So we could have solved this by just showing this file to the board and focusing on Caleb's grades." She didn't have to talk to his teacher at all. "But now Caleb's credibility is diminished. Great." She felt like even more of a fool. She handed the folder back to him without meeting his eyes.

"This is my fault," Mark concluded. "You just wanted to solve this and stand up for him and I should have told you about my plan from the start. I'm sorry."

She remained silent. There was nothing they could do now. She and Mark both agreed that it was probably best to just transfer Caleb to another school and start fresh. They would keep an eye out for the girls' progress and if anything was amiss, they would transfer them too.

"I'm getting ready for work."

Mark frowned. "You're still going in?"

She nodded. "I pushed it back a couple of hours but I should start heading out."

He nodded but just as she was about to leave for the stairs, he stepped directly in front of her and held her shoulders.

"I don't want this to ruin us."

She looked up at him.

"What will it take for you to forgive me?"

She looked down and paused for a moment before finally speaking.

"Time."

She moved to walk past him but he grabbed her wrist as she passed. She paused, looked up at him and watched as he struggled to push her for more. He didn't.

Instead he said, "I'll wait."

"Thanks."

He nodded and released her wrist when she moved a second time.

The shoot was challenging. Kristen did her best to concentrate and keep up the façade that everything was alright. She smiled and performed and assured her co-workers that her arm was fine and she was in good spirits. In reality, she felt unsettled, uneasy. For some reason, all she could think of was her mom and her resting place. She knew where her mother was buried but she hadn't been there since her return.

Why go there now?

Kristen wouldn't know until she drove there after the shoot. The cemetery was well-kept, with lush green grass and several birds humming around in the trees surrounding it. It was a clear, brisk day with just enough sun to keep her warm and just enough clouds to keep her from getting too hot. Kristen took her time as she made her way to the headstone engraved:

"Thelma Louise Johnson – Loved by all, held by God - 1945 - 2012"

Kristen kept silent. She brushed the dust off her mother's headstone, laid the flowers before it and sat silently, waiting.

Why am I here, Lord? Why bring me here? I know she's with you. What's the point of this?

Look to the right.

Kristen obeyed and pulled herself up to her haunches. She leaned over and could faintly make out the markings of another plaque or headstone only inches away from her mother's. It had been removed and replaced with fresh grass but the outline was still there.

Oh my God. The realization hit her – that was *her* spot only months ago. It suddenly occurred to her that Mark, Jasmine, Caleb, Kylie and all the friends who loved her had stood by this grave and laid her belongings to rest near her mother's grave. Mark had stood there. She closed her eyes and could vividly imagine him standing only inches away, dressed in black, comforting their children as his own heart wrenched in agony.

A thought more discomfiting hit her: what would it feel like to be in *his shoes, laying* him to rest in that very plot of ground? Tears immediately sprang to Kristen's eyes as a tidal wave of love and regret washed over her. They'd had a stupid fight, hurt each other senselessly but the difference between the two of them was that he had immediately apologized. He'd immediately forgiven her.

Forgiveness is a choice.

She was still holding a grudge instead of choosing to move forward.

Okay, I hear you loud and clear.

Kristen bent over, kissed her mother's headstone, stood up and attended to the issues of the living.

Kristen strode into the center with confident steps. She met the receptionist, who greeted her warmly.

"Do you have an appointment today?" she asked in surprise.

Kristen shook her head. "Actually, I've decided to seek treatment elsewhere. Can you please cancel all of my appointments and remove me from your list of registered patients?"

"Oh!" the receptionist exclaimed. She quickly recovered from her shock and asked, "Did you have a negative experience here? Is there something we can do to correct the situation?"

Fire Jack Vickson?

Kristen shook her head. "No. It's not the center's fault. It's my own decision for my own reasons."

With that said she turned on her heel and left the center without a backward glance, knowing she should have taken that very step months ago.

⚬⚬⚬

Kristen walked into the house and found Mark stationed in his office, his back to her as he filled out some mathematical equation. She strode across the room and wrapped her arms around his broad shoulders, tucking her face into the curve of his neck. He froze but almost immediately reciprocated, turning to fully face her. He scanned her face, a questioning look in his eyes.

"I forgive you. I forgive you and I love you. I'm sorry for being so stubborn-"

"Say it again," he rasped out. Something shifted in his eyes.

"I'm sorry and I forgive-"

"No," he said urgently. "Say it again. You know what I mean."

She then understood. She smiled at him and held his face.

"I love you," she repeated before he claimed her lips.

Her apology was lost as he crushed his mouth to hers, swallowing any objection mind or body could make. His heart soared as he relived the words she had just spoken. *I love you.* It was the first time he had heard her say that to him since her return. His hands rubbed her waist in soothing

192

strokes. She squeezed his shoulders, rubbed his back, and braced herself against the solid rock of his chest.

"I love you, too," he rumbled back in his baritone voice.

Their kisses more fervent, both of them felt an urgency they hadn't indulged in, in a while. Mark lifted Kristen into his arms and quickly carried her up the stairs to their bedroom. He kicked the door shut behind them and lowered her to their bed. Eyes locked, they undressed and cloaked each other with their bodies. They explored one another with caresses, kisses, and teasing nips. Mark traveled over the terrain of his wife's body with his hands and his lips and she reciprocated the affection. As he strummed her like a guitar, it occurred to her that Mark was a giver in all areas of his life. He gave selflessly as a father, a friend; it was no wonder he would give of himself as a lover.

Their gasps mingled as their limbs tangled. He showed her what she was to him. And she focused on pleasing him. And in focusing on pleasing him, Kristen became aware of her own searing pleasure. They trembled in each other's arms, struggling to breathe as the last rewards of their joining slowly left their bodies. Everything faded to black.

"Mom! Dad! We're home! Mom? Where are you guys?"

They woke up with a start and looked around the room in confusion. Nude and tangled in each other's arms, they realized they had both fallen asleep shortly after their lovemaking. The room had darkened and it was obvious that several hours had passed since they were last conscious.

"Uh-oh." Kristen sat up. She looked at the clock and saw that it was past four. They had slept for at least a couple of hours. Mark sat up beside her and yawned, rubbing the sleep from his eyes. She couldn't help but notice how sexy he looked with his rumpled hair and sleepy eyes. He stretched himself fully awake, got out of bed, pulled on his boxers from the floor and retrieved his pants and shirt as well.

"I'll take care of them," he murmured with a smile. He leaned in for a kiss. "Take your time."

She did. She hopped in the shower, got dressed and opened her laptop. She checked her email and frowned in confusion. It was from Ms. Walker and the subject read: "The Grade Situation." She opened the email and felt her eyes expand in shock. It was addressed to Mr. Callahan. The teacher had mistakenly sent her the email meant for Mr. Callahan.

```
Dear Mr. Callahan,

In response to your last email, I too must admit,
that I am very relieved things have gone according
to plan. So long as neither of us talks to or
engages with Mrs. Tyverson, Joshua will be assured
the top spot in the class. In light of the
attention and suspicion that has surrounded this
semester's grading circumstances, I think it would
be wise if you and I corresponded verbally from
here on out. I would also advise deleting all
previous correspondence so that our agreement
cannot be traced. You and Mrs. Callahan are our top
patrons and Principal Lane and I appreciate your
generous support of this academy.


Sincerely,
Tricia Walker
```

It was the smoking gun of all smoking guns and it landed on her lap at the eleventh hour. Kristen immediately called Mark to her and showed him the email. They printed and faxed it to their attorney who in turn contacted the academic board of trustees, and the local accreditation organization. Tricia Walker's work laptop was immediately confiscated and the school technicians were able to retrieve her deleted correspondence with the Callahans and Principal Lane. All three parties were implicated in the scheme. By noon the next day, both Walker and Lane were suspended without pay, pending "investigation into academic corruption" and the Callahans were called into a meeting with the entire board. They decided not to suspend Joshua since he had no direct part in the scheme but the parents were firmly warned that if they ever took actions to buy the advancement of one of their children again, threatening the integrity of the Academy, all four of their children would be dismissed from the school.

Caleb's suspension was lifted, his record expunged, and all of his assignments were reviewed and re-graded by a different teacher, raising his overall average from a B- to an A+. For the first time in months, Kristen saw a consistently happy Caleb. She realized what a toll this had taken on him and his self-esteem. With the ordeal behind him, Kristen finally got to know the real Caleb and she loved him even more.

July 7, 2014

It was a bright, clear day. The sky was blue and the clouds were puffy white. The excitement in the air was almost palpable as people scurried about the house, getting ready. Kristen slipped on her sleek, white summer maxi dress.

"I don't know why you won't wear the original thing," Jasmine said.

Kristen laughed. "Jasmine, it's a renewal ceremony, not an actual wedding."

She and Mark met at the center of the hall like they had months earlier.

"You look absolutely beautiful," he whispered, his eyes taking in every detail from her up-swept hair to the beautiful bangles adorning her slender wrists. He kept it casual too, wearing khaki slacks and a light blue collared shirt, his thick hair tousled just the way she liked it. Caleb wore the same outfit, a miniature of his father if Kristen had ever seen one.

They headed out to the backyard and joined Dierdra and Reed. Despite their protests, Reed insisted on wearing the full suit. "If I'm going to officiate this celebration, I'm doing it in style."

They stood before him and faced each other, Jasmine and Kylie stood to Kristen's right and Caleb stood to Mark's left. Dierdra took photos, grinning from ear to ear.

Reed began, "Ladies and gentlemen, we are gathered here today to commemorate Mark and Kristen's decision to renew their vows and rededicate their marriage to the Lord. It is my understanding that they have prepared their vows."

Mark held Kristen's hands and looked her directly in the eyes, rejoicing in the love he saw mirrored there.

"I, Mark Mason Tyverson, once again take you, Kristen Felicia Tyverson to be my beloved wife. To have and to hold from this day forward, in sickness and in health, in good times and in bad, for richer or poorer. I vow to honor, love, and cherish you. In the name of Jesus Christ, I commit my heart and my body to you and our marriage and I pledge my fidelity 'till death do us part. I love you."

She smiled, tears already forming. "I love you, too. This is a little off script but I'm going to say it anyway."

Mark waited as did the others.

"I'm so grateful for you." She looked around at their children and friends. "All of you but—" she looked back at him, "-especially you. Neither of us could have anticipated me not remembering our first set of vows or anything that happened after it. And yet you stood by my side and loved me anyway. I am so proud to be your wife."

She reached up and wiped the tears that were spilling from his eyes.

"I, Kristen Felicia Tyverson, take you, Mark Mason Tyverson to be my beloved husband. To have and to hold from this day forward in sickness and in health, in good times and in bad, for richer or poorer. I vow to honor, love, and cherish you. In the name of Jesus Christ, I commit my heart and my body to you and our marriage and I pledge my fidelity 'till death do us part. I love you so much."

Reed smiled and nodded at Mark. "Your husband has something he's been waiting to give to you."

Mark smiled and held out his hand to Caleb. Caleb proudly reached into his pocket and out came two rings: Kristen's engagement ring and her matching wedding band. She gasped and immediately held out her commitment hand, watching as Mark slid them on. He lifted the hand to his lips and kissed the finger that held them.

"Finally!" Reed exclaimed and the kids laughed around them. "Here's the best part. By the power vested in me and in the name of the Father, the Son, and the Holy Spirit, I now pronounce you what you already are: husband and wife. Mark, you may kiss your bride."

They laughed but Kristen watched as Mark's expression sobered and he leaned forward, capturing her lips with his own as he pulled her flush against him. She wrapped her arms around his neck and a potent joy filled her heart, spilling into her toes and tingling her arms. She felt lightheaded as suddenly a rush of images flooded to the front of her mind before it all went black.

"Kristen? Kristen, can you hear me? Move back - she's coming to!"

The blurry faces hanging over her began to come into focus. She blinked furiously as everything began to still around her. Mark pressed a cool wash cloth to her cheek.

"Hey," he whispered. "How are you feeling? Are you okay to sit up?"

She nodded silently and looked around at them as he helped her sit up slowly.

"How are you feeling, honey? Talk to me." Mark frowned in concern.

"Mark," she said, tears welling in her eyes, her voice choked with emotion.

"It's okay, sweetie," he said, misunderstanding. "It was still a beautiful ceremony. You just got a little lightheaded."

She shook her head. She met his eyes and tried to will him into understanding.

"Mark, I remember." Kristen looked at him meaningfully. His mouth dropped. Dierdra leaned in and frowned.

"Can you say that a little louder, please?"

Kristen looked up at them all; at her kids' hopeful faces and her friends' confused expressions.

"I remember," she said loudly. "I remember everything."

The kids exploded in a flurry of excitement, bombarding their mom with hugs and kisses that she freely returned. "I'm so sorry you went through that."

Jasmine waved it off. "You're back. That's all that matters."

"And you're cooler now," Kylie added. Kristen frowned at that but shrugged it off. She pulled Caleb into a tight hug that he returned.

"I knew you would come back," he whispered. "You promised."

"I'm glad you loved me even when it didn't look like I would."

He smiled brightly at her and let go. Dierdra nudged Reed, looking between Mark and Kristen and they rounded up the kids to go inside the house, giving the two privacy.

Kristen watched Mark as the kids retreated inside. He was looking down at his hands, a thoughtful look on his face. She laid a hand on his cheek and he finally met her eyes.

"What happened?" he asked quietly and she knew exactly what he meant.

"Things are still fuzzy after the blast. But I remember everything leading up to it. We had just finished some civilian interviews. We were getting some terrain footage when the crew was ready to call it in for the day. I remember this one villager...I had seen him before. He was a tall Afghan man in his mid-forties. I had purchased some fruit from him the day before on behalf of some of the children who lived there. They couldn't afford it. I couldn't make out everything that he was saying but he was thanking me for doing that for the kids. He said he would have given them the fruit but he couldn't afford to give his produce away anymore.

"Anyway, he had watched us while we were shooting and he called me over to him when we wrapped up. I walked over to him and he started talking about the local economy. He kept glancing at the tankard we were in and I got the distinct impression that he was trying to stall me. Then, out of nowhere, he started yelling in Pashtu: '*Get down! Get down!*' I didn't understand and I kept trying to understand. Finally he shoved me to the ground and the last thing I remember was hearing this enormous explosion and I felt this wave of heat at my back. Everything went black. The next thing I remember is waking up in that Afghan clinic."

Mark closed his eyes and shook his head in amazement. He didn't know if this would help the investigation that was taking place but he decided they would worry about that later. When he opened his eyes, he found her looking at him with tears welling in hers.

"What?" he asked. His hands automatically reached out to wipe her tears.

"You," she answered, shaking her head in wonder. "You were so *patient* with me. And loving and kind. I knew you were an amazing man when I married you but I…Mark, you were *incredible* with me."

His eyes grew tender and he shrugged. "I love you. Love bears all things, right?"

She smiled and nodded. "'Believes all things, hopes all things, endures all things.'"

"'Love never fails.'" they finished together.

"Thank you," she said. "Thank you for hanging in there with me."

He leaned in and kissed her soundly. She held him tightly, relishing the moment. When he pulled back, she looked around at the lawn and shook her head.

"What do you think that was for?" she asked, frowning. "Why would He make us go through all that?"

He shrugged. "So we'd have an interesting story to tell our grandkids?"

She punched him in his side and he chuckled, so relieved to see his Kristen back.

Mark sat back and looked around at the trees in their yard. "I don't know. Maybe He didn't plan for us to go through that but He took the pieces of a really horrible accident and turned it into something beautiful."

"'He works out all things for the good of those who love him,'" Kristen quoted.

"I'm so grateful." he said. "I'm grateful you're here. I was grateful when you didn't remember. I'll be grateful even when you piss me off."

She laughed.

He looked down at her, all traces of humor gone. "I'll never take you for granted again."

She smiled, tears flowing down her cheeks. She reached up and cupped the side of his face, exploring his eyes with her own.

"I love you," she whispered.

"I love you," he replied.

And on the clear, bright day of their eleventh anniversary, Mark and Kristen kissed again, celebrating the gift they had - a gift *neither* would take for granted again.

Author's Note

Dear Reader:

I want to thank you for taking the time to read *Remember Me*. It is my hope that you were able to suspend disbelief and escape into the lives of Mark, Kristen and their children as they navigated an unexpected turn of events. This book has been in the making since before the conception of my first novel, *Type N* but took a backburner to that novel's release. Oddly enough, I was inspired to write it after seeing a scene from AMC's *The Walking Dead*.

If you want to know more about it, feel free to email me. ☺

As stated on the copyright page, the news world referenced in the book is entirely fictitious and has nothing to do with the real workings of *ABC World News*. The circumstances and events were created to serve as a backdrop for the real work of Mark and Kristen getting to know one another again. I wanted to tell a story about the beauty of marriage, the sacrifice it often requires, and the maturity that can sustain it when two people are committed to Christ. Certainly, some may find spiritual references offensive – especially if they are not ambiguous but I am a believer and I am a writer; I will check neither aspects of my identity at the storytelling door.

I hope you enjoyed the story and I do hope **you'll take the time to write a review and let me and other readers know what you thought of the book.** Unless you're J.K. Rowling, the royalties from a book don't mean nearly as much as the feedback of the person who took the time to read it.

Please also stay in touch. Join my Facebook page to stay in the loop (www.facebook.com/authormichelleonuorah). If you want to be notified of new releases, go to http://tinyletter.com/mnomedia. Please also feel free to explore my other work via my Amazon page or my website: www.mnomedia.com.

Also, if you are a non-believer and are curious to learn more about Christ, please feel free to contact me directly. I am more than willing to share. ☺

Sincerely,
Michelle

P.S. **The MNO Media Challenge**: If you liked this novel and think that others would benefit from reading it, please consider the MNO Media Challenge by a.) writing a review on Amazon, Goodreads, and Barnes and Noble b.) recommending it to people in your inner circle – family and friends and c.) purchasing copies of this book and other MNO Media titles as a gift for others. Stories can impact lives and with your help, a bigger impact can be made. Thanks!

About the Author

Michelle N. Onuorah is the bestselling author of *Type N*, *Double Identity*, and *Wanna Be on Top?* Originally from Maryland, Michelle grew up with a love of storytelling. She wrote down some of her stories in a notebook and continued to write for fun. At the tender age of thirteen, she wrote her first book, *Double Identity*, and got it published the next year. For three years, she ran an independent magazine, *MNO*, and served as the main writer and editor-in-chief. In 2009, Michelle won the *Captured Moments Creativity Award* for her poem entitled *Encounter*. Her writing has appeared in *Vestiges Literary Magazine, Avalon Literary Review*, and *Medium.com* among others. Michelle also enjoyed a successful career as a model in her teens, walking down runways during New York Fashion Week. In August of 2013, Michelle broke several of Amazon Kindle's Bestsellers lists for her debut novel, *Type N*. A graduate of Biola University, Michelle continues to write and publish under her company, MNO Media, LLC (www.mnomedia.com). You can learn more about Michelle at that website as well as like her page at www.facebook.com/authormichelleonuorah. Those interested in being notified of her new releases can go to www.tinyletter.com/mnomedia.

www.ingramcontent.com/pod-product-compliance
Lightning Source LLC
Chambersburg PA
CBHW032004240626
47153CB00003B/1112